The Knight
Book 1: Demon

By Andrew Jamison Saum

Chapter One: The Fool

QCA, Central Band. Nov 2062

Dr Lexington Knight was a well built man, a little thicker in the stomach, but not overweight. More of a slight beer gut you could say. He was muscular, with taut ropey muscles and thick veins to accentuate them all over. He wasn't a tall man nor was he very short but a modest five foot ten. He had a handsome face and full beard which was graying in color that lent years to his young age. He had long hair pulled up and hidden under his paupers hat. He was the meditative type of person, thought well before he spoke, at least if he wasn't getting emotional . When his emotions ran he could very well easily act out. For a master, he had a personality hidden under the surface that one could say had a bit of a temper and a whole lot of jest. He was a Meta-physician with a doctorate in divinity, a healer and a teacher. He was also a Reiki Master for a few years with his own studio downtown just outside the reach of the new flooding zones of the river.

He taught meditation, Yoga, Reiki and other classes there all for free in recent years as the world had changed since The Bernardinelli- *Bernstein* Event. Of course he was always doing some work for The Arsenal, everyone was doing odds and ends for the military. They were quite busy at The Arsenal across the river. They possibly had the USA if not the whole world to save, but most likely just themselves were the focus at mind. Either way it didn't look that matters were under control.

Lex lived in a future that was considered by most to be categorically bleak. The warm life giving embrace of the Sun had left the view of the heavens in the previous decade. The reason for this having happened could be explained by some as the comet that had been in our solar system for years finally throwing an undetected chunk into earth. Causing all kinds of cataclysms, there were volcano eruptions, earthquakes and climate change. Some say all of the above being the apocalypse so many scripture had foretold of. The world was wiped out overnight. The darkness that came soon after for the survivors wiped the sun, stars, moon, and satellite communications from the world's reach.

Lex's intuition had been screaming at him lately. Lex had a famous intuition, it's what kept him alive, he just wasn't aware of that. Today something had it reeling and jiving. An event was going to happen. Lex's intuition or 'gut feeling' as he called it had a record of being about 83% accurate. This was not a good thing or made up, his brother, Gabriel Knight kept data on his 'hunches' as Gabe had called them. The numbers didn't lie. They weren't considered a good thing because they seldom involved nice outcomes. If this one was to be right they were about to be launched into something very long and arduous.

It was certainly going to be an exciting chapter. If not the last one they ever went on. It excited him and scared him at the same time. He needed the answers to so many things. So many questions were pressing him in the world let alone just in his own internal struggles. Lex and his kin were about to learn some horrifying truths about the world. Unfortunately they would not be the answers they wanted.

Since The Bernardinelli-Bernstein Event rocked the Earth hard enough that most of the world fell silent so many years ago. The world is now covered in a new dark age. Decline in technology, science, health, agriculture, species, economies, societies, and culture. Everything slowed to a halt seemingly. Flooding, climate change, the beginning of a new ice age and war were on every horizon. Was all this happening a sign of the end? The end of times.

In the middle of North America don't ask the locals in the quad city area if this is the end. They don't have time for the defeatist attitude. You can find the quad cities near the eastern tip of the Central Band as it was called. As the years wore on after the event mankind tried to pull together what they could across america. The military and what was left of the United States of America's government with the aid of its reeling people formed the Central

Band. It's the closest they've gotten to the old ways of life since The Bernardinelli-Bernstein Event. Towns and even small cities with power and water have formed under the control of the Army. The Arsenal was key in this role of rebuilding America and it was located on the Mississippi river in the middle of the country.

The Arsenal with its 15 foot walls was abuzz moving in and out organized to a level that would make ants jealous most days. Then other days there wasn't even a movement on the base to be seen. Yet, if you got close to those walls…..BANG! Most of society, at least those willing to help rebuild America from this side, worked with or directly for the Army in some capacity.

Lex continued his walk to a studio where he would get on with his day, hopefully some clients would come in for some form of help or another. Otherwise it would be back to work doing some odds and ends for The Arsenal. Making medical supplies for them in the form of grain alcohol to be used as a disinfectant while he waits for brother to get home with Ajax.

Ajax was a 90 pound three quarter wolf dog with a penchant for licking you right up the nose. This was after jumping on you to be held as if he were an eighth pound Chihuahua. Of course to look upon him was to see death approaching, yellow eyes and serrated teeth. His deep thick hollow hair was charcoal, orange and white colors. His thick staunch muscular build informed you there was no out running him.

Like most days that year it was a miserable one. Since winter was nearing the rain was slushy and its usual gray color was now almost frozen. It was as dark as the middle of night. The problem was it was 11 am in the morning. Dust and ash had fallen for years and the winters only worsened over them. Yet the sea rose and the rains fell. The earth had no balance. Not for human life, not that we deserved it either. The Earth may have been rebalancing. As far as Lex could tell humanity had spent the better part since Christ's death destroying Earth.

He finally reached his studio. Just far enough from the constant flooding of the river. The building was old. Old as in way back in the 1900s before this area was even actually considered part of the United States. Lex needed to know what was going on in the world, he needed answers. He walked through his office looking at all the scrolls, maps, books and just piles upon p iles of stuff he had acquired, all the research and work. What was it about? What's going on in the world today? Why did he think getting to higher ground was going to fix anything? Why in the end why did the Andes keep calling him? If you got high enough up in the world that maybe he could get a clear view of what was going on then? Dr. Lexington Knight was somehow bored with it all.

His Brother and he were at least going to try to escape North America as the world seemed to be going to hell in a handbasket. He'd been planning instead of excursions not only through the US but possibly way past its borders. It was just trying to find the means to be able to go on the adventure, to see what was happening in the world. To see what commits us to such darkness permanently. Let alone the lack of communications and electronics such as satellites, GPS, and telephones not working.

Lex was very deep in thought and at this moment had a very depressed feeling developing deep in the pit of his stomach. He was getting queasy like he was starting to have vertigo in his own building which was two stories high, he also didn't get vertigo. If this were a movie the ominous music would have already slowly started. This would be the point where you cue the music for the darkly lit ominous stranger who never even knocked on the door or heard creeping up the hundred year old wooden stairs.

The moment the creepy old English looking man started ambling in Lex's intuition screamed trouble had arrived. With an overly ornate cane in one hand and what seemed like an accentuated or acted upon hunched back with what appeared to be a crown underneath his cap. Was Lex hallucinating? Oh man, where was Brother?

Gabriel Knight moved as quickly as he could; he just couldn't keep up with Ajax. keeping up with 90 lb straight muscle of three quarters wolf? You just can't, Gabriel thought. Only the strong survive, he continued thinking to himself stuff like 'Darwinism and man the world truly has gone crazy, but wait'll brother hears about this'. To let him know the good news and bad news. It was really going to hit the fan, also let him know about plans getting changed things are going to get weird, quick. Lex wasn't going to believe some of the stuff, on the other hand he was probably going to. Hell he was probably going to understand it more than Gabe did. Most important part is finding out about the sunlight! How was there sunlight in Massachusetts?

Today Gabe Knight got to leave base early, to go meet brother back at the studio. Trying to get across the Arsenal bridge as fast as he could wasn't working well. This snowy ash from the early winters has made it even worse for him, military boots and an icy bridge were a non-starter. Ajax was in form as always running perfect circles around his friend. Gabriel Knight was surprised to find that the MP's at the gate had not given him any trouble whatsoever. He would not be surprised to know that there were at least three different scopes at this moment pointed directly for his head and/or heart. This was considering he was the only person and there were no vehicles going across the Arsenal bridge at this moment in the day, otherwise they would pick a few other targets to check out.

At the Studio the smell of sulfur, puke, and carnal pleasures wafting from this gentleman could be smelled across the studio at the far corner where Lex sat before the door even closed behind the old Don. The door Lex noted he never heard knocking on or opening.

The shadows from unseen angles and nonexistent obstructions made it so Lex couldn't seem to make out much of the man's face in clarity. He could see that his frame was gaunt, skin over bone. He had an air of royalty to him and held himself as such. Overly hunched as if he was hiding another small figure in his pulsating squinch under the cloak. What's with the Cloak? The man wore an extravagantly embroidered cloak with gold and purple everywhere. It was something a King or Duke would wear in the days of merry old England, thought Lex. He sauntered over slowly, swishing the smells towards Lex. Possibly towards all the plants in the various areas sucking them of their will to live no doubt.

The nausea, through all this nausea all the doctor could think of was. 'oh what kind of healing could this man possibly need? I can't even read his face, aura, manor or even his eyes! WHERE IS BROTHER!' He panicked for a moment in his head. Coming back to the darkening situation unfolding here in the now. He had to gain control and stop this, doubting his own ability to even muster the strength to help this old man.

Lex wasn't a medical doctor by any means he was a doctor in the sense of a Doctorate in Divinity and PhD in Theology, he was a Master in Reiki healing, other modalities and many other skills with belts, diplomas and degrees to go with them. Sure, Lex currently did not believe this man was living. Could this man have something to do with the state of the world? Why does the doctor smell a wet cat?

Where are Brother and Ajax? They should be here. Thoughts are starting to tear his less than calm mind apart as it becomes clearer he does not like the presence of this man. His intuition screamed at him in that moment 'that is no man!' Lex jumped out of his internal thoughts of fantasizing about what was going on around him and acknowledged the existence of the elderly man walking closer to him.

"Hello, good sir. I'm Dr. Lexington Knight. How can I help you today? Are you interested in taking some lessons or classes or perhaps there's something that ails you? I can make you an elixir or a brew that might help your symptoms today?" The creaking cackle that came from the old man was very faint and hoarse. It sounded like old brittle leather being snapped and crumbled apart in someone's hand. Lex knew it to be laughter. What is this old fool laughing at? Lex thought to himself.

"I have no use for any of those services of yours Dr. Lexington. I have another need for you. If you would be willing to take on the job. My name is Baal and I will reward you greatly. What I need from you Lex is I need you to find someone." The old man said in a voice that sounded like it had been around for a thousand years yet had the youth of a 20 year old. It even sang kind of, like there was a bell in their playing notes as he spoke. But it seemed to end with the cough of a smoker who enjoys three too many packs a day when it was done. Snapping Lex back to the moment at hand.

"Well sir I'm not exactly a private detective or police for that matter let alone the military, I don't understand why you think a meditation and reiki master would be able to find someone you're looking for." A concerned Lex said. At this point wondering why this thing came in here with a strange request to ask a meditation teacher. Everything about this befallen guy was making Lex's skin crawl he needed to get this interaction over and quickly. He was beginning to really think this old man was some kind of hellish entity. The Doctor had noticed that Mr Baal hadn't blinked once since coming close enough to monitor such a thing.

Time to get this guy moving on and out the door. He had other things, pressing matters that needed attention. Of course in comes this guy acting all creepy….. Wait, it just occurred to Lex he was going to take a closer look at what appeared to be an undulating hump on his back...wait…..did it move! From shoulder to shoulder! Or did he have a hump on both shoulders? What was going on there?

"My Dear Doctor Lexington Knight. I just simply need you to find the person who is going to use this set of cards, there are 78 of them in all. It's that simple. Like I said, I will pay you sir, I have gold, access to many precious metals and artifacts of value…....or maybe you desire a boat?..." He started coughing, it sounded like the croaking of a toad. It also sounded like the cough was thrown.

As in when one throws their voice only this starts behind him to his right and muffled.

It was an old building, with a very open studio and 12 foot high ceilings. Very well could have been an echo that bounced around and Lex may have just missed the initial casting of the voice around the room. Even still sounded like a frog, not a cough, what a strange man. No Aura, or energies? 'Maybe I'm off,' thought Lex.

"Before you protest any more Dr. Lexington Knight. Here is the set of cards" Mr Baal laid the card deck on the desk in front of Lex. It was the most extraordinary Tarot deck Lex had ever seen. It was the 78 card deck of Tarot of Mr Baal that now had Lex's curiosity piqued.

"Let me get this straight Mr.Baal."

"No please Dr. Lexington Knight call me just Baal.''

"Ok Baal, you want me to find somebody? You don't know who? Somebody who is going to use this deck of Tarot cards? Are they? And you're going to pay in gold or valuable artifacts, maybe a boat, to do it? I got to know what's the catch?" Lex had to come around from where he had been behind the desk so he could inspect the cards "May I inspect them Baal", Said Lex suddenly hoarse. The thought of gold and a boat, That would get him out of North America. But, how do you find someone today?

"You may." purred Mr Baal. Lex was about to touch the deck of cards when he noticed that they were not your ordinary deck of Tarot cards. He also noticed there was the sound of purring coming from behind Baal over his left shoulder. The Doctor did not have a cat in the studio.

Lex looked over one of the cards he had picked up, it felt powerful in his hand and whispered softly to him promises of glory and riches. It was The Fool card, arguably the 1st and last in the Tarot deck. The most potent and the most destructive. They were in the manner of Tarot cards but they were uniquely individual in the sense that he'd never seen anything like them. They had a cuneiform or runic style writing he had never seen before around the edges. They depicted demons on them instead of trumps or the usual cups and swords.

Broken down into a normal 78 tarot hierarchy and they were utterly dark and yet gorgeous. They had the most beautiful writing that slowly changed. Lex's eyes slowly started to understand the writing. He quickly averted his gaze from the writing. There were all kinds of subtle symbolism in the paintings on them. Simplistically beautiful artwork that seemed to move and talk as you gazed at them. Lex threw the card down on the table with a bit of longing in his heart. It whispers to him of adventure and unbound knowledge. He felt a migraine coming on as an aura appeared in his vision. Why that card he thought, of all the cards, why that card?

"I don't believe I can help you Mr Baal." Lex said, rubbing the bridge of his nose with one hand.

" I know you can help me Dr. Lexington Knight and I know you will find the person that can read those cards." Baal insisted while taking a few steps closer. Lex heard his steps thanks to the cane on the floor and moved back a few in response.

"But sir, they're written in a language I've never seen before" Lex was looking around the room. Then on his desk with one eye on Baal. His nerves were on fire.

"It takes a certain mindset and concentration to be able to read those. I believe you'll see in time. Dr. Lexington Knight I mean you no harm. I need you to understand I'm not here for trouble." Right at that moment he started croaking-coughing again and it had a language that sort of came out of it that was odd. At that instant his back started to heave. There came rhythmic motions under the ornate peleg he was wearing. It was undulating and pulsating with more life now.

"Are you okay?! Mr Baal!?" Lex's stern voice said to Baal as he turned to help "I'm very concerned you look sick, why don't you sit down and I can look you over!?"

"I'm fine Dr. Lex! You're not even an actual medical Doctor, you're a Meta-physician, I am damn Fine Dr. Lexington, But thank you. I'll be okay. I just need you to find someone for me! That is all." He seemed to have screeched it like a cat, where did your melodic voice go Mr. Baal? Thought Lex. Visibly stressed out and struggling, the man was trying to keep his cloak on. He also seemed to be working his way closer and closer to Lex

Time to make a move, thought Lex. He is getting too close to me. I should do it. His mind reeled with consequences of what he was about to do. What if he is just some old man? And not an actual threat to me? His thoughts raced. A plan started to shape as he stared at the small palm sized crystal ball on his desk just a feet away.

"Well, let me take your coat for you," said Lex right as he grabbed at the english rag of a jacket from the man who now seemed charged with unseen energy and nimbly moving away from Lex

It didn't matter, Lex was quick enough. Leaping for the coat as there was a squealing like a cat mixed with the croaking sound of something of the deep abyss. At that very moment the front door made its usual dramatic slam opening. A loud crashing bang against the inner wall made for cracking the old plaster far too the upper floor. Gabriel Knight and Ajax had made their entrance. Lex jumped at the god given distraction. Grabbing the perfectly circular crystal ball off his desk he swung his body back towards the old man.

As brother came crashing in his usual style, way too excited, yelling and running with Ajax. Through the door Ajax came full on sprinting in his doggy parkour fashion. Running around Gabe and halfway up the wall then back onto the stairs. As soon as he got to the top and turned the corner he saw the situation instantly determining his move completely on animal instinct, loyalty and the trust in his best friend and master.

The coat came flying off of Baal as Lex used his left hand to rip it finally away. Three heads! The demon Baal had three heads, one of a cat, one of a toad, and one of an old man. They all screamed in unified terror. Lightning crackling in the air all around the room with sudden and intense demand to the evil energies at work. Darkness danced around him as he started saying words in cryptic tongues. Words each one of the heads seemed to be lashing out at all three of the targets in the room simultaneously. The targets being Lex and his kin.

Which is exactly when the inner child of Lex released that middle school pitch he had readied with the solid quartz crystal ball roll. The crystal ball went crashing into the frog's eye and exploding into a spasm of icker and blood everywhere. The results were screams so piercing that everyone's ear drums started popping with the horrifying sounds from the outcome of the attack.

In that very same moment Ajax lunged at the cat's head biting it around its neck. Wiping and ripping at it till it started a series of explosions of black igor and pus in all directions. He pierced its vital areas over and over with horrifying screeches deafening the air even more. With the weight of Ajax in full momentum pulling down on the middle of this top heavy beast of a demon. Burying down and forward to bring it to the floor. Only to find out that this old bastard was too strong. Blood and igor sprayed from the throat of the feline's head. It wailed as if dying in solidarity.

Brother had finally made himself to the top of the stairs, the shock and awe the situation had sent his mind reeling almost to a point of cracking and at the same time into a surreal belief. Then he snapped out of it and his soldier instincts took over. Lightning hit the roof as it was flying out from every direction of Baal. The roof started to collapse. Gabe Knight started to move as fast as he could but it was too late. He hit the top of the stairs as the roof collapsed upon his legs and pinned him there. All he could do is try to unbury the bottom half of his body while watching the battle unfold in front of him. Having no idea how, or what any of this was.

The wolf Ajax struggled with Baal in a pile of rubble. Lex was by the desk still and all the cards spread out before him. Lex was shaking off the chaos as he tried to steel himself. He looked at the mess of cards now unfolded everywhere. Their images danced and spoke to him. He picked one of the cards up. The card slowly revealed itself to Lex as he was staring at the hieroglyphic writings in the border of the card. Slowly he could see the words, then he could read them. "The cost of one cycle commands him for one task."

As Lex read this it was too late the card started to melt. Crashing through the roofing and centuries old building ripped the heavens and hells of dimensions no mortal man is ready or wishing to visit. Lex couldn't believe he actually had pulled that card out of all cards and read it. It was too late and here came Azazel of the Tower card. Lex wanted to avert his eyes but he couldn't as the portal opened further and its horrific yet beautiful dimension was to be seen. Then the figure slowly came into sight as he descended fast to this dimension. This could be seen through the slit in time and space that was above them. This rip in THE ALL in this small Davenport Iowa building.

  Azazel descended, you wouldn't have thought he was a demon he looked like one but he carries himself in regal. He was lit with fire and flame energies that could be considered godly and the flames came from everywhere. His face was that of scorn and screaming as that of a conqueror. Living eternally screaming Goats heads adorned each shoulder like paladins with curled horns that would impale any man who dared near him as he sliced through the hordes of anyone who opposed him. They spit flames, as did everything or area of this unseemingly angelic demon. Sword flaming as he ascended down upon the demon Baal in the studio of the Knight's. Speaking in tongues so foreign, so loud Lex's earum started bleeding his thoughts turned mush.

  There was nothing else for those moments, it was beyond something of meditation, there was nothing other than thunder, fire, pain and the awe of Azazel. The wolf Ajax released his death grip from the cat's throat with a popping sound that turned slosh and ended with a sickening splash. Running away bloody icor all over him. This utterly horrifically orgasmic entity of a thing looked and turned its gazing endless depth at Lex speaking in a voice that swore only the utmost allegiance, loyalty and praise to whomever it was speaking.

"What do you wish for me? Is it to do with little Baal the toad?, Or shall I help you rule this realm?" Azazel's voice was most angelic voice Lex had ever heard

"Take him back to whatever rock he belongs to." said Lex in the commanding tone of one who should be in charge of such things. He suddenly had an urge to impress Azazel.

"And what of me Sir?" Lex somehow enjoyed the melodic voice of Azazel

"Away to your home Azazel, and I free you on one condition." Azazel, having gone from very pleased, suddenly very upset. Not that Lex could tell from his aura he didn't have one. Not that he could tell from any training at all, it had nothing to do with NLP or any kind of reading whatsoever it was plain as day Azazel was pissed at the word condition.

"What is your condition Sir?" he sang.

"Well azazel my condition is based firstly on knowing about these cards, you're tied to it if I don't free you is that correct?"

"Yes" The world around them didn't seem to move at all. All except for Ajax the wolf who had taken cover.

"If I free you from this card can I call you friend, foe or a favor owed"

"You may call me none, you may call me Azazel" Has the melody in Azazel's voice disappeared?

"So if I do not free you from the card you still have to do what I say and back to the card you go and I can call on you again?" Lex was beginning to be concerned for how much time he had in this state of transition with the demon Azazel. He had never been frozen in time before. It was beginning to make him uncomfortable.

"Yes" Cimed Azazel, fire and lightning appear to move so slowly they were almost frozen in spacetime around them. A spectacular light show of brilliant reds, oranges, yellows and whites stood minutely still in the world around them.

"Last question, what is the cost of a cycle?" Lex's eyes never left that of the Demon Azaels the entire time the demon hovered in his presence.

"One year off your life, Inconsequential, if you have to use the cards you are going to die anyways without their use. The choice is simple for your kind, it always is" There was mirth in the demon's voice. Azazel was smiling at him. For a demon covered eternally on fire he was handsome.

At this point the whole room seemed to be frozen; nobody moved, looked around, or breathed. Not even the lightning seemed to be crackling in the room anymore; It was hanging in the air silently like decorations. It was just as if Azazel and Lex were having a casual conversation over the outcome of the situation at hand. For some reason this talk like it or not Lex was enjoying it more than any conversation he had in the last 11 years of his life.

"Azazel, return him to whatever place is hell and as for you, you're free. I am the card reader now and your service to the cards ends here." Lex didn't like these cards. He knew he was stuck with them now, the best move was to get rid of them one by one.

They were gone with a swirl of fire and dark smoke only to be burnt out in embers and ash. The smell of brimstone laced the air that Lex smelt while laying there in the destroyed building that was once Lex's business studio. He could hear his brother coughing and yelling for him.

"You okay brother?" He heard a faint but steady voice reply.

"I'm good but what the hell just happened man?" Before he could even turn to see how Ajax was doing Ajax was there licking his face and jumping all over him. Then turning his head to look to the right he saw a huge pile of some random looking artifacts, a few buckles, a brass bottle, copper, lead, gold and the spread out cards all over his wrecked floor in front of what was the destroyed office behind it. Dr. Lexington Knight was well aware of what had just occurred. He knew the horrors that were going to come. All he could do for the moment was lay there and feel like THE FOOL.

Chapter Two: The Emperor

OCT 1st 2062

The Studio had been destroyed in a frightful battle. What was reported as a lightning strike that caused a fire. That is the end of the story as far as the local news went. That night passed and the weeks went by. The brothers found themselves a comfortable home on the hill above the East Village. Dury old Iowa's the East Village, Mount Ida East Village formerly Camp McKinnon and Camp McClellan throughout the centuries. Now partly a city and partly a station for the Arsenal across the river. Most Likely to be a war camp once again soon.

The house was one of the older homes. Not the oldest there were homes here that had been built in the early 1900s before it was even the United States. This was one probably in the 1930s and then some renovations in the 1970s. It was old and looked just as new as the day it had been built. Supposedly a three bedroom it was not a very comfortable one considering it was a two-story shotgun style house painted natural Earth tones of browns and beiges. They were not bland or derrie like one would think; they were actually more warming and inviting. Not the abusive assaults on the eye Lex was finding them to be at the moment.

Lex lost everything he thought was his life work with the studio near old downtown. He enjoyed the place where he helped a lot of people in his days there. Not as many as he could have if The

Event had not happened. He had been near The Source Bookstore, all the soldiers' housing and The Arsenal. All places he needed to keep things afloat business wise.

In the weeks since the building was destroyed his brother approached the Doctor for several missions with his Army unit as a special contractor. This was not unusual in these days and times as able bodied men were in short supply. They offered much help with this building situation. They were not going to fix his building but find the doctor a new one to resume his operations again. Lex has spent his time trying to figure out the mystery of Baal. Lex was sitting in the office at home pondering all these things.

Then it dawned on him everything his brother had explained to him over the last couple weeks since Baal's appearance occurred. How unbelievable. Sunlight in Massachusetts, near Salem. What did it mean? It meant they were hitting the road and soon according to Gabe. The mere thought of it all sent Lex's mind spinning. That area of the Country is under water. We have known that for years. It's also considered a dead area. It is near what was once one of the most war torn parts of the county.

Lex looked around intently at his home office wondering what his next move was going to be. He had to tell brother about the cards and about Baal, The Demon King. But he didn't even know what it meant fully yet. This was going to be difficult. At that moment he heard a croak; the croak of a toad. Before he could say oh shit a demonically croaky voice came saying the words.

"Good day there old friend. I bet you have a lot of questions?" A hideous toad his tongue wiping out at flies. Flies that were manifesting from its own back via popping boils of its flesh. Its purid body, producing many such boils as they actively burst out these horrid little flies. Wearing an ornate golden little crown upon its head as it spoke "How nice to see you? How is Lex the doctor? That most powerful card reading Magician's. What a ...." A boil popped and a pure black fly buzzed out of it only to have the toad lash a tongue at it and swallow it. Blurpping in pleasure. "I never meant you harm Lex, why did you attack me?" it burped again. More flies were swarming around it. It's tongue eagerly lashing them up.

Lex jumped up into a chair grabbing the large tome he was gazing at off of his desk and tossed it instinctively onto the floor forcely. It slammed onto the toad squashing it into a ooze that leaked from around the edges of the large scholarly book. The old wooden chair creaked and bowed then finally broke into pieces sending Lex to the floor with a loud crash that jarred him. His head was cut open by the chair and bleeding everywhere.

"Is that anyway to treat a friend?" another toad croaked as it bounced out from around his desk to look at him sideways while targeting and tounging a fly.

"How are you and I friends in any way? And I suggest you be careful being a toad in this house. We do have a cat here." Lex struggled to get up off the floor; he was all tangled up in his own robe and the broken chair. It started occurring to him that he needed to hear Baal out before reacting. Maybe he should be in a chair sitting still. He started to control his breathing and slow down. If this Demon wanted him dead he would have been dead. It was time to hear him out. Then react.

"Oh I assure you Doctor, Matilda is quite busy at the moment cleaning herself in another room and we are well alone at the moment." a new toad croaked making a little hop that made its crown tilt to the other side.

"I'll try not to take any of that as veiled threats or warnings of harm in my own home Mr Baal. or shall I use another card to smash you as a toad?" Lex was gonna play tough and show the demon he was not taking any crap. Not in his own house. That would have to start with the questioning.

"I hear your brother got you the great news, what wonderful news it is learning about the Sun shining in Salem. Fascinating stuff. You're going as well my friend, good…good. We need to talk about all this, you know….Salem, I'm a lot more involved in all this than you think Dr. Lex." The demon left the last part out there dangling.

"The last time we spoke there was a fight and you destroyed my studio, leaving me cursed with these cards. I wouldn't exactly call that friendly Baal." To accentuate his sentence he smashed the frog with the left heel of his foot and a putrid squish spewed organs across the floor. Hoping to show the demon he meant business when it came to talking with him. Knowing that wasn't the end of it, Lex tried to prepare himself for what he needed to ask and how. He sure seemed to know a lot about what was going on, especially Salem. What did he mean? He was more involved.

Lex continued to cross the room looking for another book to continue his research or possibly smash a toad. He was getting ready to plan a trip to see what was going on in Massachusetts, supposedly Salem. The military had recently commissioned him to go along with his Brother and his team and find out about these lights and the possibility of sun showing in certain parts of the somehow newly rebuilt city of Salem. Everything around Boston and north is quiet and littered with villages, that is, the parts that are not under water. Everything south of New York is war torn or nuclear.

MOP or The Men of Pride are a group of men who came about in the early 2020's. They originally were more annoying than anything. Then as time went on they got bigger and bolder. They started off as a radical white supremacist group hiding as politically motivated militas who were here to protect the American dream. Over the next few decades they turn into domestic terrorists. After the world went dark, they were able to organize what remains of parts of the south into their ranks and now use them to try and take over the remaining people and resources to rebuild the states in their ideal way.

Meanwhile all over the country people are starving and dying of disease. People in the USA fight with each other just from village to village for food in some states. It is real chaos in some areas and the military is doing what they can. They have control and support from the local population here in the Quad City Area known as the QCA and in what is called the Central Band. They have pulled together in this Central Band across America slowly connecting and rebuilding a network. Lex was learning a lot in the war journals from the eastern front. Recently he acquired a large set of intel from his brother in preparation for a mission to scout if anything about Salem is true. Most came in the form of handwritten war journals. Some from before The Event.

It was an exciting time, which is why he had no time to deal with demons or whatever the hell Baal thinks he is. Let alone a putrid toad that can talk. After retrieving an atlas of the world circa 1647. He could smell it before he even turned around to see another toad popping out of the dark shadows. Flies appeared as they popped out of the boils from his back. It's tongue lashing out as it spoke.

"And now that wasn't very nice of you to do there. I thought you were a humane person and a master of your own emotions." If a toad could smirk this one did. It's a little crown wobbling on his head as if it was chuckling.

Lex full-out kicked the toad all the way across the room and it hit the wall and slid down with a sicky black slime left behind as it croaked out its last breaths. Two more toads could be heard when they plopped out of the shadows one side each, left and right.

"Gosh, well Baal what do you think? What do you want? How about stop being gross just talk to me?" Lex was saying this as he reached for one of his old baseball bats in the corner.

"I can't help being gross, this is the way I've been made. It's the only way I can appear to you now. I'm going to keep the two toads in case you decide to destroy one, or stop wasting things, like I don't know, say the card of Azazel? Setting him free. You shouldn't be freeing demons from the cards. You're going to need them to get through all of this and Azazel was important. Do you know the history of his? Do you know what you've done?"

"You entrap me and you come in here after you tried to kill me and my brother and you're trying to tell me what I've done! How dare you? As far as I know you're nothing more than a hidden one! Or one of the Great Deceivers from another dimension! Who simply claims to be a God caught in a Demon form or a deity. Nothing more than an entity from another dimension that means nothing other than to be a prankster like that of Loki. You claim to be the great Baal. I've seen no greatness from you other than a curse and some cheap parlor tricks with lightning, so be quick with your words. Before I am gone with you through one of these cards again!" Lex's anger was coming to full display and that rarely happens.

Baal was thoroughly amused with this but trying not to let it be seen and he was also too preoccupied to realize what was going on. Lex had been swinging up a bat at the end of his rant. A swing he fainted, the bat right towards the one toad that was actually looking at him and it started to jump backwards. But it was a faint after all and Lex turned fully swinging the bat back to the left side toad who was totally unexpecting it as it went smashing into him sending him across the floor in a smear of sticky black blood.

"There, now I feel a lot better." Lex leaned the bat against the wall and sat down in the closest antique chair he could find. With a light squeak as old as it was it held his 215 frame just fine, his muscles a ropy tense mixture of veins and fibers were pulsating with blood. His breathing, rhythmic and deep. You could tell he was using methods to keep himself calm even though you can see the fire in his eyes was still there, yet it was laced with a little bit of delight of having smashed another one of the putrid toads. "Worry not Little toad. I'm not going to crush you. We have a lot to talk about. I have many questions that you have lots of answers to. Let us start with the Azazel since you seem to be so upset that I let the one demon who didn't belong in that pile of cards go."

"I am the great Baal! I was worshiped by the Canaanites. I am a great deity of fertility, agriculture and wisdom! I can turn great magicians invisible! I bring great things! I bring the lightning and the thunder! How dare you question who I am, you're nothing but a peon in all of existence compared to Baal!" He roared with sparks of little lightning around the toad for effect.

Lex stood up and grabbed the bat from its position leaning against the wall. "Then why do you need me so much, little Toad!"

"I didn't try to kill you Dr. Knight, you attacked me, I simply offered you the cards and asked for help…." The demon toad left those words hanging there. Lex sat back in the closet chair. He signed long and low. Thinking to himself of the situation. He looked at the Demon.

"Why do you need me Baal?" Lex left the words hanging there and for a few mins and the two just sat there staring at each other thinking.

After the conversation, which was a long one. Painful and full of fighting and making little black messes all over his home office. It had been well enough Lex needed to drink and he needed one bad. He decided since his brother sounded the same way on the radio that they would meet up in the village pub for a drink. He also agreed to speak with the demon in person and hear him out more later. Lex was going to meet his brother then speak with the demon in person.

After radioing that they should meet in the East Village pub for a cold one and discuss plans. Lex and Gabe were down in the

East Village inking at the local pub. It was basically the encampment center where you can find the stockade, the blacksmith, shops, the restaurant, local gathering areas, sitting areas and post office. They like going down drinking, telling stories and listening to stories of the soldiers and locals. Just laughing away the night and the problems they had as well as the problems other people had.

They had been there a few hours before Lex was getting tired and decided he was going to walk back home. He needed to get some sleep. He had a lot to do in the next few days and he was pretty sure it was about to get a whole lot busier. He turned to Gabe Knight and told him as much. But Gabe was really deep in his cups. His response was barely audible through the bar noise but he could make out the fact that he was going to sit and see if he could figure anything out from the engineers. They were in need of a few more bodies for the excursion to the city's new bridge site.

The Corp of Engineers had recently blown holes in the sides of the Mississippi valley north of the QCA for the new bridge. This would take the train across the river and straight into the Arsenal from all the factories they started to rebuild. In the process they opened limestone caves and collapsed the side of a major bluff. Many Died. Stories of monsters attacking and killing people in the area, especially anyone who goes in the caves followed quickly after. The Military naturally is not happy and wants this taken care of to get things back on track. One Major Lightfoot had plans on how to maintain the schedule.

The Doctors walk home had been dimly lit by electric lamps. They lit the road here and there. The moon didn't offer much light other than a faint glow behind the everlasting darkness of the black clouds and smoke that covered the sky permanently. Lex talked to himself about how one day these damn skies will bring back the Sun. This can't be the end of it. He continued walking the brick road, admiring the night air even though it is smoky and mostly the smell of decaying wood and Earth. Then came the peculiar smell, something familiar, a familiar rot in the air like a sick disgusting perfume. Smelled like Mr Baal the demon must be close.

It was almost an insult to call Mr Baal a demon though. Of course the definition of demon had lost its initial meaning to Lex in his studies he'd come to learn that the demonization of angels, gods, deities, powerful beings and entities throughout history is what demons really are, to a certain extent. Then there are the Djinn, the hidden ones, Faeries and the unveriversal Con men as well. Baal could just be a misunderstood one of these and well be a product of hatred turned into a demon by other religions and people.

Right on time an old man wearing a very nice Leo coat came over the hilltop. It had all kinds of embossing and embroidery of the finest gold lace craftsmanship into it and he walked with a cane. He had a little limp, he wore a crown like cap on his head and from what

Lex could tell he had one hellish grin on his face as they caught eyes with each other. Lex couldn't help but smile a shit eating grin on his own face. Mr Baal screamed with elation "How wonderful to see you Sir!" throwing an emphasis on the word sir as if to accentuate the fact that he was not a human man.

"Didn't I just get rid of you?" said the drunk Doctor leaning far over and pointing at Baal sideways. Baal on the other hand 'planned this timing perfectly' he thought. He was looking down a conversation with a half drunk Doctor Knight on his way home, preferably this is perfect in his eyes as the Doctor would be a little bit more pliable to the words that were going to be spoken to him.

Captain Gabe Knight meanwhile was still getting deep in his cups in the village. All on the pretense of working on recruiting and intel. He'd been talking to local soldiers trying to gather information on what was going on at the new bridge site. From what he would gather were tales of demonic women. At least that is what the soldiers who had made it back would say. Flying birds like condors or mutated animals were attacking any engineers and then the soldiers guarding them as well. They are trying to fix the new bridge site so that the train can start to ferry across the river north of town and into the Arsenal. Gabe Knight was having a hard time believing anyone. Maybe because he was deep in his cups and many sheets to the wind. Plus the stories were unbelievable to begin with. Naked mutated women with wings flying or mutated birds striking from above and killing combat trained soldiers and engineers. Hell the engineers are highly trained soldiers too, it was just all unbelievable. Harpies killing soldiers in Iowa, come on he thought as he slammed another beer.

He raised his hand to get the bartender's attention but it was hard considering how busy it was that night. Not just the attack at the studio lately but many things have been going on. Words from across the world, and in the country where things were burning. Men of Pride recently attacked local outposts around the QCA. The military was catching heat for not defending it. Civilians had died. Gabe was of the opinion that they should go on the attack and wipe out the Prides, the military was budding with other plans.

Meanwhile both of the evening's conversations with Baal had been more than overwhelming for Lex. He had learned a lot about Azazel, the fallen Angel turned Demon. Azazal's story had its roots in religious Judean mythologies. The Achdemon is king of the Seirim, goatlike spirits. He spawned the assyrian guardian spirits known as Sedim. The fallen Angel was later exiled in the desert chained to the trees till the end of days as punishment. Interesting words to be heard at 3:00am from a centuries old man in a crown and cape, when you're drunk.

The conversation earlier that evening before he was drunk had most of the Azazel conversation. But what interested Lex was how involved Baal was behind the military looking into Salem. As well as the inclusiveness of one doctor going along. It appeared the old man himself was actually very high up in the military and he had his eyes set on the Knight brothers. There was something he wanted that he could not afford to lose or have out of his hands much longer. Baal had said that near the town of Salem the witches had come across something we needed very much. The only problem lay in these magicians who had taken over the area. A proud order of men who he seemed very disdained to even mention. It was all so much to take in that his head was spinning by the time he got home he passed out in a drunken whirlwind of nightmares.

While Lex was sleeping little did he know his brother would be visited by one Major Lightfoot. A man he had just crossed pathways with on the road. Unbeknownst to Gabe Knight this Major was actually Baal in disguise. To Gabe it was Major Lightfoot and The Major was just there to have one with the soldiers. Probably to see if they were getting ready for their trip to the new bridge site as well. Baal wanted to have a couple words with Gabe. Gabe, filthy deep in his cups, went to a corner of the bar to sit with the Major and have a chat about the mission. This should have seemed odd being 3:00am in the morning and nine sheets to the wind.

Unbeknownst to Gabe the subliminal messages and spells that Baal was secretly slipping into his head during this drunken conversation were strong when mixed with the drugs. Drugs he had sl ipped into his drink while they talked throughout the night. The two things in conjunction were going to begin the very long and slow slippery slope into madness. A trip that would be Gabe's undoing, leading to his ultimate fate. But it was required nonetheless to push Lex the direction that Baal required. The fate of the Knights was in his hands.

The morning came quickly and there was not a bright dawn. In fact it wasn't much lighter than the night since the sky was always dark. Lex was hungover to say the least. He was pacing around the house wondering where Gabe was; he had not returned home that night. Gabe had been drinking profusely and Lex was worried this was becoming a habit. His encounter with the demon Baal on his way home did not leave him thrilled with what the possibilities for Gabe might have been. Lex was aware in his eyes that Baal was not interacting with Gabe. Although the opposite was the truth.

To try to calm his mind he went to his botany room and tended to his plants. He wasn't the world's greatest botanist but he did try hard. With the help of technology. He had several high powered LED lights and misters as well temperature regularization all aiding him in his grow room. He proceeded to roll himself a mixture of sage, marijuana and other herbs to relax his nerves. Also open his brain waves if you asked him. He was preparing himself to go into a trance. He needed to seek other worldly advice he could trust and there was only one place he could go. Lex had deep rooted grief over his mother's untimely death and had his own way of dealing with it.

On the other side of the river Gabe was waking up in the barracks closest to Command. He felt he needed to walk home with some of the engineering contractors he had met. He went home to pass out in their barracks. He managed to recruit quite a few for the mission. He had walked back with them to make sure in the morning they had not changed their minds. Also to walk them straight over to get orders issued from command. This shouldn't be a problem considering the bridge was a priority; they just need bodies in the engineer department. Luckily Gabe got these contracted ones to sign on and hopefully their current orders wouldn't conflict with the new ones. If they did they would just see what Command could do about moving orders around. Major Lightfoot said he would make anything happen for Captain Gabe Knight and assured him he was to be Gabes ace up his sleeve if anything stood in his way.

Waking up was easier said than done for Gabe. The concoction of spells, drugs and liquor had his head pounding. He rolled off his cot and hit the floor with the sum of 270 lb of pure muscle and hungover. The lightning pain that went from his head down his spine and back up again forced a thrust of vomit that projectiled across the floor and under the cot the otherside of the aisle. This one move began a chain reaction amongst the soldiers who had all been drinking the night before that would go down in history in that barracks and amongst the troop of men. Forever known it was the morning of horrors.

Gabe would find no problem getting orders issued later that day. Or getting the barracks cleaned. The supplies they needed, the transportation or even the ammunition and guns. Baal had seen to everything as he was going by Major Lightfoot on base. All of this was unknown to Gabe as he could not see Baal for who he was, no one could. Only Lex could see Baal for what he was. This is how the king demon wanted it. It would be a cold day in hell before anyone saw his true form.

Lex had a special contractor designation with the military through Major Lightfoot. This ensured that he would be able to go with his brother on these expeditions. Especially to Salem. Their first stop would be to the new bridge site just north of the Quad Cities, an area apparently now fraught with danger. Reports of attacks from the Men of Pride and now mutants coming in attacking civilians and soldiers alike. Plus you had your regular old river bandits and scumbags who are trying to jack anyone coming up and down the roads in and out of town that has supplies. Anything from medicine, food, and you name it was valuable these days. People were just trying to survive and some of them were going about it by any means necessary.

Lex was in a dark room sitting in the lotus position on the floor. Eyes half closed staring into a large oval shaped black obsidian mirror. The only light in the room was from a long stick candle that was placed behind the freestanding obsidian mirror's stand. Both the mirror and Lex sat in the middle of the room. It was completely silent and the darkness enveloped everything except for the shining liquid black surface of the mirror. Lex was deep in a trance-like state that was getting deeper and deeper as he concentrated on his breathing and he soft focused on the liquid of the mirror as it started to swirl. "Mother?" he asked out loud softly .

Chapter Three: The Chariot

Gabe slowly approached the house with Ajax in tow. Ajax was doing circles around him sniffing things, peeing his way around marking trees and old dead cars that sat there rusting away. The pit of Gabe's stomach sank as he got closer to the house he knew he was going to hear from Lex this time. All he wanted was to take a shower, his third one today. Pack some clothes and sleep before they have to hump it down to the train yard. They were going to take a train and three Humvees. Go up to the location of the new bridge site. He was hoping he could get there without much of an argument from Lex since his head was still pounding and his body aches seemed to intensify with each step closer to the house. It was seemingly easy how he got off of the army base without much of a problem. Major Lightfoot had been a godsend. With all the help he has provided Gabe as far as moving any and all obstacles in his path. What a great transfer from the east the Major had been.

He opened the door to their home, it creaked showing its years. He thought to himself I've got to get some WD-40, oil that son of a bitch. Before he could close the door he heard Lex yell "Is that you brother?"

Ajax bolted past him with his tongue hanging out of his mouth bark after bark as he ran deep into the dark recesses of the house grabbing at a chew toy he ran off to play in the corner.

"Yes brother, it's me. I stayed at the base last night, sorry I didn't radio it was about 5:00 a.m. before we left."

"No problem dude. upstairs packing stuff. Were you able to get any engineers together and when do we leave?" Lex was packing very little; he was actually trying to get the mirror away before his brother saw it out. He didn't want to share that he had been scrying again. As the conversation always leads to arguments. His brother thought it was a useless form of managing grief. That Lex was actually compounding his problem. Also that he most certainly was not contacting the soul of mother. In fact it made Gabe question his brother's sanity. The same could be said for how Lex felt about Gabe's developing drinking problem.

"I got several civilian engineers to join us as contractors. They were already working on the base, so I went back to the base with them and had their orders switched this morning. We're leaving tomorrow. We're going to the new bridge site first and will be there several days before we head East." His voice was shaking and hoarse. His head pounded and he felt a new wave of nausea come on.

Lex could tell by the sound of his brother's voice that he'd been drinking and probably up to that very moment. He wasn't going to push the subject. Lex just had a long talk with their mother and it had gone very well. As well as one as one can interpret messages from passed souls. He wasn't going to share that information with Gabe just as Gabe wasn't going to share much of the information he had with Lex. Their relationship was strained this way. There'd been a lack of sharing this way since their mother died. Secrets, they would be keeping secrets from each other that would ultimately cause rifts. While Lex was thinking about the things his mother told him his brother slipped into the bathroom and closed the door as a sure way to be left alone. Lex knew he wouldn't be seeing or talking with Gabe anytime soon. It hurt him inside.

Later that day Gabe would be sleeping off the tremendous hangover. While he was in his nightmare hellscape throughout the day in his room. Lex would be elsewhere. Lex desired knowledge, knowledge of these demons tied to the cards. They seem to be mostly demons of Solomon. Directly from The Lesser Key of Solomon to be exact. Azazel and a few others not of the key were here. But all 72 of the Spirits in the Key were in the cards.

Lex is headed out to the bookstores. Books were a hot commodity again, cable television had gone by the wayside years ago. In fact most devices and communication stuff above the cloud coverage is a no go. Nothing above those charcoal black clouds ever gets through. Makes it a hard run for books too. Hard to find the ones you're looking for at least. Especially if they were rare when cilivision was at its height, like Lex is currently.

    It's only about a mile or so to downtown and it wasn't that bad out that day. There was not any real slushy snow falling yet. What had been out there wasn't really impeding his progress; it wasn't too cold, just a bit of a nip in the air. Lex decided to take Ajax with him since a wolf is a great companion for walks in this day and age. He was great off the leash and stayed close to far away as needed. Plus he was an amazing deterrent for local crime as no one wanted to mess with a wolf.

    The two of them walked along happily, almost skipping between them. It wasn't an amazing day, it wasn't even a nice one. One would wonder why the two of them were so happy and pleased. Realistically they were just happy to be alive and excited to be going somewhere. Since everything had happened they were stuck in the quad cities, stuck under these clouds, stuck with the same reasons and answers people had given them. Now was a chance to go out and find some of their own, maybe get new questions and answers. Whatever, it didn't matter, it was a call to adventure.

    The weight of Baal the demon and whatever ties to the cards he had been given or been enslaved to here recently didn't seem to affect him at this moment either. Even though Lex had gotten zen with the idea of the cards rather quickly. It was because like the darkness of the sky, he had no choice. He was aware he could just never use them. There was also something about everything going on that was just filling Lex with life again.

Right at that moment he tripped, fell straight on his face busting his nose wide open on the corner of the sidewalk. It was bleeding like a river. There was blood all over his face, shirt and splashed across his peleg coat. It was just running down him in droves. He sat in a cold wet pile of mushy ash riddled snow with blood running down his face and chest in between the fingers of his hands. Laughing hysterically with Ajax licking the side of his head and nudging his way into his armpit. Lex was laughing at himself; that was life. Everything was great with him, so he has to trip and fall right?

Lex was too busy laughing to hear the man named Mikey approaching from his left side yelling and screaming nonsensical things about "How he'd been wronged!" and "Hey you! Mr why are you laughing at me!" This feral crazyshit covered, half naked poor homeless person did not see Ajax on the other side nuzzling into Lex. A mistake he would never forget. Lex Intuition was going bonkers but he was too busy laughing to care, He thought to himself. "I know to look out for the curb, I got it already, stupid gut feeling."

A shit covered hand reached across at Lex and grabbed him by a handful of his long hair pulling him viciously towards the exposed belly and crotch of the feral man. At that very moment he was ripping Lex's head down a scream released in agony from the Doctor's lips. Ajax's head coming out between Lex's armpit and arm only then to be seen by the man pulling Lex's hair. A snarl coming across his face with a low growl deep in his throat, Ajax lept.

The nightmares were just the beginning of the trip into madness for Gabriel. He found himself in a dark mysterious place, smokey and smelling of sulfur. He looked around for signs of life or markers to show where he was. It was unlike anywhere in the world he had been. It was a twisting maze of black and deep blood red rock. Often twisting so much that it came back on itself. He crossed his own boot prints in the ground more than once before the screams started. That's when the panic started to creep into him.

The screams were horrendous. They came from all directions, layered in the hundreds. Cry's and pleading. Voices of all ages. They all screamed in agony as they yelled for Gabe. He could suddenly feel them tearing at the other sides of the walls trying to get closer to him. Did they want to help or to hurt him he couldn't tell.

His stomach sank as the screams and clawing sounds intensified. Sweat was covering his body and dripping off him everywhere. The heat and humidity in this place was well past tolerance levels for the average person. Gabe started running as the panic in him grew. His soldier instincts told him not to panic but they also screamed for him to run for safety. He now felt he was in the most danger he had ever been in. He turned his head only to glimpse the most disgusting creature he'd ever seen. It was several humans all melted together into a mass of limbs and mouths screaming for Gabe, crawling and clawing towards him.

"Help us!" They hissed off in unison. It sounded like a bad echo in this chamber of horrors. Darkness and fear gripped him. Gabe's horror was complete when he recognized some of the faces of the creature as it got closer. They were people he had fought alongside. Soldiers he fought with and for. Soldiers who had died. His terror was complete; he couldn't run; he was petrified. His mind was frozen as well. It told him this was it. Hell had come for him.

With a couple words Ajax released the man from his death grip. Blood running down his face and dripping to the pavement. Ajax sat at attention, anxieties high but sitting as still as possible eyeing the man who attacked his master with disdain. The man rolling in pain and anguish. Blood filled the gutter with bright red color as it mixed with the water from the melting slush. Lex grabbed the man and tried to help but he slapped him away and continued his death roll in the gutter crying and bleeding everywhere. Lex had only a few moments to save this man before he would bleed out. Thinking fast he did the only thing he could think of. He knocked the man out cold. Ajax let out a loud bark. Lex turned to Ajax ``Bring me Gabe boy!" Ajax was off running before he even said boy.

Gabriel woke screaming covered in a cold sweat, his arms flailing grabbing for safety of anything as he jetted forward and up, he was halfway out of the bed before he realized he was awake. His breathing was heavy as if he had been running a marathon. The dream felt so real but that's how dreams were. Doing his best to shake it off, he got up and started walking around his room not sure where he was going. He was rubbing his head muttering to himself. That's when Gabe could hear barking. It sounded like Ajax was on a tear outside. He started looking for clothes.

By the time Gabriel had finished getting dressed the barking was very loud and right outside in the front yard. He'd rushed up the front stairs but it was too late. Ajax reached the front door and slammed into it. If the door hadn't been locked; it probably would have swung open. Instead it made its customary loud bang. That was how Ajax made his knocking by ramming into the door till someone answered or it opened. Gabriel opened it before there was a second bang. Ajax was there splayed out on the ground barking to follow him. It was obvious he was needed somewhere, for something had happened.

Gabriel ran for the Humvee parked in the driveway. Ajax ran off past it toward the corner street half a block down. Gabriel kept an eye on Ajax's movements while he started up the Humvee. It made a loud roaring sound with a low pur as it evened out. He popped it in reverse, wishing he had thought to combat park earlier and pulled out of his driveway turning back around to follow Ajax and turning right at the next block. The Humvee had no problems on the beat up old Davenport streets. These roads in the East village were brick. Which made them even worse when they were unrepaired, not that Davenport was repairing the roads anymore anyways.

    Turning right on 9th Street and heading down the road he could see Ajax just as he headed up over the hill and was going down towards the river he pressed his foot on the gas and heard the echo of the Humvee on the bricks as it roared him through the hills. Gabriel thought to himself "I'm on my way brother"

    Gabe came to a screeching stop mere seconds later over the small hill as on the next corner was Lex hunched over a shit covered man in a scene of blood and gore everywhere in the dirty frosty covered corner. It matched the red brick road nicely. Lex yelled "Help me Brother!" showing his blood covered face and chest as he turned to face the humvee.

    "Jesus man! What the hell happened!" Gabe's response came from the window as he opened the door and pushed the release for the back to open. "Looks like you guys tried to kill each other." He ran for the rear of the vehicle to retrieve the medical kit.

    "He attacked me out of nowhere. He appears to be one of the local feral homeless." Lex was tiring his best to keep pressure on

Mikey's neck wound as best as possible. Gabe was already halfway to them.

"Didn't see Ajax." it was a direct statement of fact as he was looking at the wolf dog. Ajax was covered in blood himself and sitting on the dead grass not 10 feet away awaiting any instruction of his master. "They never see you, do they boy". He sat down on his knees next to the man and started to administer first aid with the help of Lex. Captain Gabe Knight suddenly calmer than he had been in months, maybe even years. Lex noted this, he had never seen his brother so still, such a master of himself. He watched him with more intent than he ever had. Gabriel was a combat Medic in his original tour as a soldier. That was many years ago, but it was something he was truly good at. He worked quietly and confidently away on the man only looking away or speaking to instruct Lex to assist him. The entire operation to get the man stable enough to move to the hospital only took a few mins. It was some of the best few minutes Lex with his brother lately. The thought saddened Lex's heart and brought weight upon his soul.

"Ok Lex stay here a second and don't let him move. I'll get the cart and we will get him in the Humvee to get him to the hospital. What about you, are you okay?" The calmness was gone and Lex could see the slight shake in his hand return and the hollowness to his eyes return.

"Yes brother, I am great. Just a bloody nose. That was an amazing job man! You were awesome!" He went to high five his brother but was met with his back as he had already turned to go to the humvee. Lex knew he was not happy. It surely had more to do than with this. He loved saving the day. "What's up man? You just saved my ass and that guy's life? And you look like someone kicked a puppy, what's up dude?" Lex had the most serious of expressions on his face as he then started coughing loudly and uncontrollably. The conversation stopped at that point.

"Brother is that?" A concerned look came over Gabe's face. Worried that Lex had the Black Cough. Lex looked his brother in the eyes, Gabe turned away to get in the Humvee.

"I'm good Dude, I don't have The Cough, that dude just messed me up good." Lex resigned himself to the conversation being over. Gabe was starting to wall Lex out.

Their relationship showing how strained it was really was becoming. The unspoken part was quietly eating at them slowly. Gabriel was clearly hurting deep down and needed help and Lexington knew it. Lex just did not know how to help. If Gabe walled you off then that was where you stayed. Lex was going to have to find a creative way to help his brother. Lex didn't want to ask his mother but it was probably the best place to go for advice on the matter. At least for now. He had just spoken with her that day and it had not dawned on him to discuss the finer details of his relationship with his brother.

The brothers trip to and from the hospital was uneventful. They enjoyed the time together laughing and talking about plans for the future. Plans to leave the country, see the world. Plans to find their grand adventure. They had no idea it had found them. They should have been discussing plans, cards, demons and Salem. Instead it was nonsense like Like the goofy Private Cameron Gunner. Lex did manage to get a ride to The Source bookstore downtown as Gabe was headed across the river to the Arsenal to check on the orders for the engineers and the mission to north of the QCA for the new bridge.

The military was building a new bridge just for trains north of the city. A route for them to directly enter into Arsenal and right up to its new subterranean areas. In the past 20 years the expansion of The Arsenal has been paramount and most of it in secret. Those secrets have also been all out of sight and underground. Since the skys went dark and the world went blind the military went tight and pulled inward to the states. Command of the government and military is broken into two sights: the 1st is in Colorado and the 2nd is here in The Arsenal.

The news of sunlight in Salem has the Military preparing to mobilize to the east to find how and can it be replicated. As well as to take over the area and instate control. Considering the Central

Band was always meant to reach fully across the USA as a dividing line to use to rebuild outward from there. It worked fine into their plans. The United states government is still around in a sort of pseudo-state government. They are under the state of Colorado where the entire government of the USA hid and remained hidden to this day since The Event. With the military spread and hidden in other parts of the world in the same manner. Arsenal being the 2nd biggest one. In plane sight and completely unknown to anyone.

They continue to operate under the same laws and views as before. Even holding sessions and elections most of this unknown to much of the USA due to the lack of any communications system and war. Some would later argue it was done this way to maintain power in a select few

The reality is the chaos of a worldwide cataclysm in a time of rampant distrust and disinformation lead to small vacuums of power and trust that destroy any chance for anything other than complete chaos. Added that the government is trying to retake the country from its bunker that they ran and hid in? From The Event they never warned anyone else about? This wasn't true but the people didn't know that.

This was all fuel the Men of Pride were able to use in their resurgence as a relevant force in America. Let alone they were becoming an army. People didn't care so much about the past now as they did about surviving. The one thing Prides were giving people who were far away from the Central Band was safety, shelter and food. Not to mention the living conditions. Further away you got from the Central Band the worse conditions got. Less running water, working electricity, and access to medical care. Prides were controlling that line between wastelands and promised lands. The area between chaos and order.

Chapter Four: The Hermit

The Source book store was the oldest operating retail store in the downtown area thanks to flooding and what seems like the collapse of society. This 100 something year old book store was still going while hundreds of other businesses had come and gone around it. It was family owned and operated since 1939, not always by the same family. But never by a corporation. They deal in rare and collectible books. It was a hallmark in Davenport if you asked Lex.

Downtown was now old downtown and it was holding on with the constant war in the south and apocalyptic climate change changing the landscape of the country. Things were moving uptown fast, which was the New Downtown. The area of downtown was for the business of soldiers mainly who live here and work for the Arsenal. New barracks on the lower hillside in the downtown area formerly lofts in previous years made for this new way of life in town. The new size of the river helped with its extended sides and new flooding zones. The family somehow kept the store running amongst all this turmoil. They had many customers, like Lex and all the soldiers who came and went. There was no longer Tv or even really that much radio left. Books were invaluable in some cases and priceless to some people.

It was an old building on the main drive. It was darkly lit inside which was terrible for a bookstore but the owner supplied a flash light if you needed one. The Lines feeding the grid here from the Hydro electric dam were suffering badly. Lex was a regular and lame enough to have a headlamp on hand when he came. Today Lex would be looking for anything he could find on witchcraft, magick and demons. He was going to try to look without having to inquire about anything. He wasn't exactly sharing with people that he had to find away to protect himself from demons. Even though the current man running the store, Dom, was a family friend.

Lex couldn't imagine it would be easy to find books on demons that would be helpful. In fact he was sure the only sure thing he would find would be rather useless. If anyone had anything or knew where to get it, it was The Source that was for sure. Lex jumped up out of the humvee at the corner and proceeded to walk down the street towards The Source. It was always windy, wet and foggy downtown. It was starting to lightly snow ashy slush again. Lex pulled his coat tight and held his hat with his other hand. His leather messenger bag swang on his shoulder in the wind as it picked up.

Lex noted the river was only a block away these days. Making its flooding that of epic proportions. He jumped a little when he heard voices. Turning to see it was just a few westenders that were always done here. Lex was trying to remember their names. The westend of Davenport was full of colorful personalities and free spirits. These three young men had a few encounters with Lex and they were all playful in nature as Lex recalls. They may get in trouble but they were no harm to Lex. In that moment of thought he wished he hadn't left Ajax at home. He suddenly felt very alone. He gripped the bag containing the cards and put his arm in and held them.

What a weird reaction he thought. To reach and hold the cards at a moment's notice of fear? He understood the comfort they provided and the power they made him feel was what he imagined is close to a god. He felt near invincible when he had summoned the fallen angel Azazel. The control he felt over a seemingly hopeless situation at the time. One he now knows was not so dangerous. In fact he was the one who caused the danger if anybody had. Baal claims to have been there to offer a deal about the cards and Salem. He says he never intended to hurt anyone and he never does. At least not the Knight brothers. Still he didn't want to be in any situation with a demon and he certainly didn't want to be summoning them. But there he was with 77 demons left.

To get out of the mess he would need knowledge. He would also need to move forward, as in with the demon's plans. Lex figured his way out was most likely tied somehow in the actual plans Baal had laid out for him. He was just going to need to figure out those plans. First he would need to figure out Baal and the cards. From there he could best find his motives as he traversed whatever path he has been thrust upon.

When he spoke to the spirit of his mother she made it clear that he needed to get to Salem to escape the demon. She cryptically warned him about Salem. Mostly she stayed clear of the subject of the town and stayed on the topic of knowledge. She said she left her books with Rod by the river and that he could find them there. So apparently she had sold books to Rod at the The Source bookstore down by the river long ago and they were still there. Lex was in need of witchcraft and Magick knowledge. Something he glazed over in his metaphysical studies as mere fantasy and things of the past. Sure certain methods proved true over the years like scrying, but Magick and witchcraft? In its oldest and true forms? Why not believe he did have demon conjuring tarot cards after all? His mom sending him to get back old grimoires she sold was just not sitting right in his stomach. Something was off about the message. His intuition was speaking again about the message. He had something wrong.

The sudden smell of downtown filling his nostrils with the scent of dirty river water and rotting buildings was enough to wake him from his internal questioning. Questions he kept asking but already seemed to have answered. It was just that he was getting too comfortable with the wrong parts. He was gonna find what mother sent him out for and then he would catch brother up to speed on the scenario by showing him. He just hadn't figured that part out yet.

He walked up to The Source bookstore while looking up and down the road, his eyes stopping on the three boys again. He opened the door with his left hand and released the cards with his right and removed his hand from the bag as he entered. "Hey Dom!" he said enthusiastically as he walked in and passed the low counter, walls of books to both sides of him. The walls reach to the far blackness of the darkening rear of the store.

"Well hello there Dr Knight, how are you doing sir?" The older man smiled warmly at Lex for he was genuinely happy to see him. He slowly sat up from his seated position behind the counter.

"Oh Dom don't get up for me and I have told you hundreds of times you can call me Lex." Lex moved to help Dom at the end of the short counter space by placing a hand on his elbow. He was met with warm eyes and a frail y hand on his. It was a nice moment between old friends. "Just you Dom?, where are the youngsters at?"

"Oh Lex, you know off with some of the other guys meeting about some project, just being young I guess, I don't know how you do that these days." His eyes seemed to glaze over at this thought. Lex changed his focus to the man's aura, he could see the thought was making him feel depressed.

L ex didn't know what to say to make him feel better other than to just change his train of thought. "I need some books on rocks and caving if you got anything? I am headed just outside of town to look at some caves for my brother's team." Lex knew Dom loved Gabe and the Military. He didn't need any caving or rock books, but this would make the man's day.

"Hot Dog Lex! A mission to caves with the Team? We better find you something helpful I cant send out there looking like the fool with those boys" The old man perked right up and Lex finished helping him out from around the corner of the counter. Lex was hoping he could work on his true motives while they hunted for caving and rock books. "Rock climbing too I bet?" Added Dom full of new energy and grabbing his own head lamp. Dom knew Captain Gabe Knight well as Dom's youngster brother was on Gabe's team and had died in a vehicle wreck on a training weekend. Something Gabe blamed himself for to this day.

"You got it Dom, anything that can help me keep up with them in the caves will be mighty appreciated. I imagine if rocks are in the title it can help me." They giggled at the last little joke. Firing up their headlamps they started the small talk and looked through many sections of books. They went through more sections than needed as was their ritual. It was more about talking and finding the occasional lost gem of a book than anything.

They had five books in tow and were talking for almost an hour before Lex started to argue in his own head about just inquiring for the books he never saw anything remotely near what he needed. It was only Dom after all.

"Hey Dom, I have a question about my mother maybe selling some family books to Rod that worked here a long time ago? This will sound weird but they were Grimoires, Like personal family journals? Sold to Rod by the River is all I know. I just found a faded note at home in mom's things" Lex felt relieved asking about it now that he had. He questioned his internal anxiety.

"Oh boy Lex, no you got your information wrong you want to see Lady Rivers, you're mother was friends with her I bet the note or whatever you got, that there are books or what not is meaning it is with her. They were best friends. They had a New Age shop together many decades before The Event. Let's get her address for you. She is not that far from where your house is Lex." He had a warm smile and disposition about sharing the information Lex had noted. He wasn't sure how asking about witchcraft was going to be received. Lex hesitated asking earlier because he wasn't sure who was okay with what views these days. It was really hard to tell. He had to hide his practices from his own brother to avoid conflict. And Lex was just a spiritual guru with occult tendencies.

The rest of his visit was uneventful other than his gut feeling talking loudly about something he hadn't figured out yet. He had a few books and a solid lead on where to go for mothers things. He didn't want to wait on Lady River till after the bridge site. Lex was hoping he could squeeze a visit in with her before they left.

Lady River was a high Priestess of the River Coven and a very potent witch. She was skilled in the ways of divination and had seen Lex coming. She was preparing her Imps and familiars to tend the house and grounds. She was a Beautiful round old lady with curly shoulder length gray hair. She sat back in a rocking chair with a knit blanket over her sipping an herbal brew. She had deep crows feet and round dark brown eyes. An inviting smile on her face.

She whispered into her pinky ring and a swirl of inky smoke like aether formed in the air and shot out a three and half foot tall Imp. He landed nimbly in front of her

"What can I do for my Lady?" He sang as he did a bow til the point the tip of his long nose almost hit the ground. Szuil had been a friend and sworn Battle Imp to Lady River for over 70 years and he would be till she died.

" Szuil , my old friend. Will you please help clean and prepare for a special guest? Evelyn Knight's youngest son is coming by for a lesson." She smiled at Szuil acknowledging a deep relationship between the High Priestess and the old Imp.

"Of Course my Lady, Should I prepare the sandlot and cauldon areas?" he smiled, adjusting his little tailored suit as one of the buttons had fallen off. He was trying to pin it in place while maintaining eye contact.

"No, just the sandlot pit and please acquire his mother's effects from my room." She rocked back and forth. He stopped playing with the jacket. The Imp wondered if it was wise to take on another witch to train at this age. Especially Lex. Why not have one of the other priestesses do it? The Coven did not lack skilled witches who could handle training Lex. Maybe Lady Rivers just wanted to train her friend's son herself.

Szuil stood in the candle lit room breathing in the incense and herbs though his large nostrils as he signed. He held Evelyn Knight's Book of Shadows, other strange grimoires and a two and half foot Cold Iron Casting Rod in his small outstretched hands. He signed again. He saw what his Mistress saw when she gazed into the future so he knew about the fate of Knights and the real dangers that surrounded the choices Lady River would make. He trusted her, it was that he was just tired. So old and so tired. He looked around the witches room, it was full of dried herbs hanging amongst charms and trapesters. Candles and incense burned everywhere, there were protective and calming peaceful signals all over. The room settled you into a calm state, almost euphoric. He enjoyed breathing it in one more time before turning and walking out to tend to his tasks.

As Szuil walked through the old large home it seemed empty for most of the Coven were away on duties or personal errands. Szuil was going to need help so as he walked through each room he picked up random seeming objects. A decorative bottle here, a belt buckle there. He recited spells as he went that made it sound almost as if he were singing. The spells were simple incantations and the like that Lady Rivers had set up for turning on the lights and opening windows. Basic things these little spells to help with daily life and easy enough that the Imp could recite them some even in his own Impish language. Szuil had several objects in his hands at this point and decided it was time. He brought them to his Mistress.

Lady River was rocking away in her chair whispering spells to a black cat so that the familiar could carry the spells throughout the property to be fulfilled. Szuil came shuffling up with arms full of trinkets in his outstretched hands and Lady Knight's effects swung over his back. Lady River laughed at the old Imp "Do you think you have enough friends there?"

"Can you?" he retorted slyly with an equal smile and mirth in his voice. opping several of the enchanted amulets.

"Well why not Szuil , It is a special guest and it's been a long time." she said while opening a little bootle the sudden swirl of purple sparkling smoke surprised no one. Neither did the bang that followed. What was left in the aftermath made them smile. A pot bellied Imp was laying there in a buttoned up suit sleeping in the dead grass, snoring away.

"Should we let him sleep?" Szuil whispered to his mistress

"Depends, do you want to clean the circle yourself?" Lady river quipped while rubbing a belt buckle. Smoke started to appear in the air around her and you could hear a voice in the distance yelling "weeeeee!" and another imp this one only a few inches in size appeared as if riding a roller coaster out of nowhere. Down the side of Lady Rivers and the front of her. Around down her legs through the smoke and trailing it as he came into full generation. The whole time yelling weeeee. Much to the enjoyment of all but the sleeping Imp who didn't so much as roll over.

"Ok you two help me wake the others and prepare the manor for our guest, please" Asked the High Priestess with a chuckle in her voice. Lady River enjoyed the company of her Imps very much.

River Manor was an old home settled into the hillside overlooking the great and mighty Mississippi river. It was high up on an overlook near Prospect Park. With a round drive through driveway and wide grand yard that was hidden in the great hill by very old trees. A yard that was large and hidden from most eyes. Lex lived only mere blocks from River Manor and had no idea it was there. That was the idea though.

Back here hidden from view of the river and all but the back porch was a massive area with a few fire pits. More than one pit had a great caulon over it, the pits had tables positioned closely on one side with shelves and jars for easy access to ingredients. All of them in the shape of a circle save one in the shape of a triangle. The final area was an open stone circle pit of sand. Each stone had a different symbol etched into it. Massive brass braziers in the four carnal corners lay unlit. It was here that battle magick was taught and where they would prepare to see what Lex and his demon cards could do.

    Gabe, parked the humvee in the driveway, Ajax was running circles around himself in the lawn next to it barking and turning then rolling and barking. Gabe grabbed the bottle next to him he had acquired from the PX. He figured between Lex almost killing his old friend Mikey and the errands he said he was going to run, Gabe had some time to drink. Maybe try to catch some more sleep. Gabe was supposed to be at the base and running his own errands or at least that's what he told his brother. He had no such thing to do and he had no intention of doing anything. He was going to attempt to take the hottest bath he could and drink his bottle of midwestern hooch. Then going to the blackest sleep possible before they left for whatever hell tomorrow is bringing.

    Ajax was barking loudly rolling around in the slushy ash earth. "Dang it Ajax" thought Gabe. "I'm going to leave you outside for Lex to clean, that'll buy me some more time to sleep." Gabe jumped out of the Humvee, put the bottle down on the ground and started to wrestle a little bit with his buddy Ajax. Trying not to get too muddy as he was wearing his only clean pair of fatigues.

After wrestling with Ajax for a bit and growling at each other. Even smiling a little. Gabe went to the rear of the Humvee to pull out his weapons and hump his gear inside; he didn't need any shifty people stealing his gear in the middle of the night. After pulling it all inside and taking slugs off the bottle he proceeded to take a hot bath.

Gabe locked the door to the rooms behind him. He ripped off all of his fatigues. Jumped into the hot bath with his big old bottle of hooch and proceeded to get drunk. The only sounds he could hear was the running water and the sound of Ajax enjoying himself outside in the yard just below to the left window. The room steamed up with a constant stream of hot water flowing. He all but drained the bottle. Alone, in a bathtub.

He put his gear away as nicely as he could for someone who was in a stupor. He staggered outside and fed Ajax. He smoked a couple cigarettes he had stored away while finishing his bottle. Then he went off to his bedroom to proceed to fall asleep to a series of horrifying nightmares.

When Gabe woke up he looked around. He was somewhere on base. It was very dark and he could hear the sound of electricity and sparks. It was the flashing in the foreground he heard the Major and he proceeded to walk towards the sound. Hitting an unsettling feeling as he moved forward. Sounds of electricity got louder and louder the yelling of the Major deeper and deeper. The walls closed in further and further as he went it seemed to get tighter. The air got thinner and it was harder to breathe the closer he got the sound of the Major's voice. Something told him he had to get to the Major's voice.

He turned to look behind him and something was after him he couldn't see it off in the distance. It was dark that way but it was huge and hulkling. Oh my God was it that mass of melted bodies again. He couldn't even start to deal with that thing again. His hands started shaking violently. He turned and tried to run in the direction of Major Lightfoot's voice but his legs wouldn't go. His legs were fatigued and he just could barely walk. The oxygen was so thin in the air his muscles weren't receiving enough is what he told himself. He got to the end.

The light was coming from the corner just as he heard the thing get closer he turned right. There was Major Lightfoot where he went to say something he couldn't say anything, just a loss of his voice. Gasps for air. He grabbed for the Major's shoulder as he did. He could feel something grab for his feet and legs. His mind was scrambled eggs he wanted to scream. As his hand got on the Major's shoulders, he turned and looked at him. His eyes were hollow and his skin was gone. There's nothing but muscle and gore.

"Welcome Home Captain" came the Major's greeting in a hoarse voice devoid of all emotion. Gabe couldn't respond and there was no oxygen left. There's no muscle in his body left working. Gabe couldn't move at all. He could feel from behind whatever horreden monstrosity was there upon him. Fear and horror gripped his mind. He looked down at the majors' chest, his hands reaching for his stomach. The Major's hands were nothing more than a tangle of writhing serpents all scrambling to get into Gabes stomach and tear at him. Hissing and snapping violently for his flesh.

Gabe woke up screaming terrified, covered in sweat and trembling. He vomited profusely all over himself in the bed. Continuing projectile vomiting to the right and over the floor. He sat there shaking. They seemed all too real to him.

Chapter Five: High Priestess

Lex approached his house coming slowly up the old brick road noticing that none of the lights were on or any fires outdoors, indoors or furnace or otherwise were burning. This meant his brother passed out early. A Humvee was in the driveway so he was certainly home. Chances where Gabe was drunk passed out as this seemed to be the norm lately. Suddenly movement caught Lex's eye from his left. Then from the dark came out of nowhere Ajax, fainted an attack on his master. Then ran off in the other direction towards the house. Lex made chase laughing. "Come on boy. I'll get you!" he yelled, laughing.

He was glad for the distraction his canine companion had brought. His mind was going to a bad place. He didn't know what his brother was doing and chances are he could just be tired. Things have been crazy lately. He had no right to assume the worst or box his brother in like that. It's not like he was any better; he was struggling with grief too as well as messing with demons and witchcraft. Not exactly sharing that with anyone either.

Lex was playing tag with the dog in the yard noting how dirty Ajax was. He took him around back to the hose and water buckets. Then started hosing Ajax off and decided he'd walk with him over to the Lady River's house with him. See if she wasn't maybe home to talk to. He can always send Ajax back home if the dog wasn't welcome.

While he cleaned the dog off he came to the spot where Mikey's blood was. Mikey was the name of the homeless man that had attacked them. He found out a lot about the man at the hospital after they dropped him off. There he was more to Mikey than just a local crazy homeless person. He had not always been that way. It was just after The Event that things went bad for him. "Too bad things had gone down that way they did when he crossed paths with us." Lex thought. Ajax started licking his face and his tongue went right up his nose as if to distract Lex from his thoughts again.

The Doctor started laughing and pushed the dog away. "Come on you bastard," he said laughing. "Let's go meet Lady

Rivers." He pushed up off the ground, grabbed his bag off the nearby meteorite mistaken for a stone. He checked for his things inside, took one look back at the house. Still no activity as far as lights, movement or sound. He sighed to himself.

"Looks like we have a few hours before it's pitch black out" he said to his furry companion. Ajax who was deep in stretching suddenly stopped and stared hard and long at his master. Turning his head slightly, his yellow eyes narrowed. He barked twiced. Tagged Lex hard with his nose and ran as fast as he could leaving torn hunks of dirt tossed in the air as he shredded off. The game of tag had begun again.

Lex didn't miss the look for he knew it well and before Ajax could even start his forward jolt to tear off. Lex had tagged him back. The sheer madness of the move had the dog going bonkers. Ajax instantly started to protest the tag back by barking and running in circles around Lex. Lex laughed at his friend "I know, I know. I cheated. But, you were running in the wrong direction anyway."

Lex would be the 1st to admit that his scrying sessions interpretations were questionable. But he would also be the 1st to tell you they were factual. In the sense they had happened. Now if you can unravel the riddle of information you get from the person you get it from is another thing entirely. Information he received from sessions with his late mother always seemed to work out eventually. This last session was a perfect example for such a case.

He started at The Source bookstore by the river and now he was at River Manor who his mom used to own a new age bookstore with the owner apparently. 1st part done, now for 2nd part. Rod and grimoires. Ajax was licking himself and leaning hard into Lex's leg. They had been standing across the street from the Manor for a while just staring at the old and foreboding Manor. It was massive with so much rich detail and character. Painted greens and earth tones with so many statues and hand made sculptures around the yard. It was lit up, obvious someone was home and they seemed to be expecting company or at least they had the welcome mat out. It had a wide drive with a large yard that overlooked the Mississippi river on one side. All this yet it was hidden to all who didn't venture down this little side street.

Lex was working on his breathing when Ajax jumped up and ran off toward the house. Around off into its massive back yard the wolf ran the whole time Lex yelled for him. As he was yelling for Ajax and stepped into the yard a voice could be heard in his mind

"Hello Dr. Lexington Knight, I called Ajax to the back for a treat, I hope you don't mind? You two were taking such an awful long time. Won't you please come join us?" The voice was calm and sweet like his mothers was. As he walked slowly through the yard he started to smell food and sweet herbs and spices. His mood changed as the air did from rotten earth and wood to that was the sweetest springtime he could remember as a child. He closed his eyes remembering a time when the sun shone on their now sickly skin.

He unbuttoned his peleg coat as he came around the side of the house. The yard opened up to this immense area of many uses and broke down into many sections. There were even old unused areas for gardens. There was so much to take in, amongst it was a series of fire pits and a sandpit. Between the last fire pit and the sandpit sat an old woman in a rocking chair, swaying back and forth in her chair. She hand fed Ajax some kind of meat that had been roasting on the open fire nearby. At the fire a black caulon was being tended to by a short little man in a weird hat. Lex wasn't paying him any attention though as he approached the round old woman.

She was wrapped in hand knitted blankets. She had the warmest of faces and deep almond brown eyes. Her face had many deep wrinkles that spoke of many many years on earth and unbound wisdom. She reached her right arm out in greeting. Much like a Queen would have. As she did, the dagged cuff of her dress fell all the way to the ground. It was lacey and well crafted finery.

"Greeting Dr. Lex Knight I am the High Priestess Lady Rivers, Welcome to River Manor this is Szuil my highest level Imp and assistant." She waved her hand majestically to the right to show the man he so slightly noticed earlier by the pot. The Imp turned around with a little shuffle to come into full view.

"At your service Sir." Szuil did a little bow that made his very long ears bob up and down as he went, as well as his long nose all but touch the ground. Lex fully saw Szuil for what he was now. An actual Imp. It wasn't a short man. He was taken back and started to back step while muttering something. His hand went into his messenger bag reaching for the new found protection of the cards. Szuil looked at his Mistress "Mum." he said with more than a little stress in his voice.

"Lex, get a hold of yourself in my Court, you will not need such things in my home….. Lex. Lex!" she yelled his name at the very end with an enchantment for effect. Lex shook himself free and released his hand from the cards. Why did he grab from them in the first moment of panic, again?

"I'm so sorry Szuil and Lady Rivers. I Don't know what came over me. I am only human. So I react as such. I have only read of such things as, Imps? My dear friend, is that correct? You both must bear with me" Lex reached in his bag again this time calm and he pulled out his glasses. Putting them on his head and removing his fedora. He moved closer, reaching out a hand to shake. "I'm Dr. Lexington Lex at your service Szuil you may call me Lex. Pleasure to meet you." He turned and greeted Lady Rivers with just as much excitement, this time bowing deeping at the mistress. Extending an arm wide to the side with his hat in his hand. With that she invited him to sit down for dinner and a very long conversation.

Lex enjoyed a long meal with Lady Rivers with several of her Imp friends. Ajax played in the yard with her familiars. Lady Rivers and River Manor had many familiars and Imps staying with the Coven. It was a very old Coven and had acquired many magical assistants over the centuries. Witches can live much longer than normal humans but Imps and magical assistants that come attached to amulets or of the Fae or Sidhe variety live many centuries longer. It's said the oldest Covens have 100's of these companions if not 1000's staying in their Manors.

Lex learned a lot about witches and Imps as well as his connection to a long line of witches in his family on his mother's side at dinner. He learned of the connection to nature in the world witchcraft connection to magic in general is a natural thing. They talked about his coming journey to the north just outside of town and the need for this bridge. The Lady seemed very interested in the idea of them digging in the side of the river for some reason Lex noted. They discussed the mystery of the Arsenal and its push to expand so fast when it seems people are still picking up pieces since the Event cast rot on the world.

It was when he brought up his mother that Lady Rivers got distant as her eyes glassed over and her mind wandered. Lex could tell she cared deeply for his mother and that Evelyn Knight had been very close to her. Evelyn apparently had not been part of River Coven but was affiliated with them. She was a friend but an independent witch. She did join them in various rituals like festivals and sabbaths; not an official member as the coven was and typically is full. Lady River also cited she was quite an independent woman and in no need of other psychic energies to draw upon. This brought into their conversation of psychic energies and her ability to talk to Lex in his mind. Her powers only ranged so far into her domain, but she was indeed a strong psychic and powerful Witch.

They discussed divination skills at length. As his mother was quite apt in them. Lex was just learning to dabble with his scrying mirror. Lady Rivers offered to help Lex and his developing skills. Lex eagerly accepted. The two of them were beginning to build on what was going to become a very solid friendship as Lady Rivers was beginning to see it. Lex, lightheaded and wary of it all, knew the subject of the demons was this coming back up as they took their conversation back to the yard. Ajax was in the yard playing with a rather large bobcat named Lavi, a familiar of a River Coven witch who had been living near the Manor and was an old friend of theirs. They wrestled and chased each other roundabout the yard playing. Not a care in the world. Much too Lex's surprise was the fact that Ajax was a familiar. Lady River had been surprised to see that Lex had no idea. "You thought a wolf just friended you?" she laughed at him. Lex stood there watching the dog and cat play.

Lex was trying to make sense of the fact that it already made sense. It was a wolf. He found, friended and domesticated a wolf when he was in his 20's. He had crazy strange intuition powers. The list goes on if he wanted it to. Mom was a witch and so was he. It was not hard for him to come to terms with ideas that felt so natural to him. He was walking towards magick training areas for a session on circles and a demo of the demon cards. This was what his gut was telling him the other day. Destiny had found him. There was a side knot in his stomach still talking to him about Lady Rivers and he couldn't figure it out.

Lady Rivers had handed Lex the two and a half foot cold iron rod and grimoires after dinner and told him to proceed to the sand pit she would meet him there. They had spoken about the grimoires at length and he understood it was up to him to read through and understand the magic that they hold. She could guide him from there. She has been very insistent about her offer to train the Doctor in the Craft and he has accepted. It will just be up to Lex to show up and do it now. He started for the sand pit with the rod and his bag in hand.

Watching Ajax chase several cats and a Bobcat in an out matched game of tag. It was a sight to see. Ajax slipped and rolled wildly into a giant puffer mushroom and it exploded, trillions of spores into air like clouds of gas. Covering the wolf in a carpet of dusty spores and goo. He howled and shaked aggressively before returning to the chase of the nearest feline.

The butterflies in his stomach were going nuts the closer he drew to the fire pit. He could feel the heft of the rod in his hand. It was made of cold iron. It was a mystical iron that fell from the sky. Hammer beaten into a rod that was imbued with magical powers for casting. It was a powerful magical rod for a battle magician. On one side a quarter length down its edge was sharp as a razor but unnoticeable until touched upon. On the other side it was lightly beaten to have textures so that the hand could feel it as a grip but it just appeared to be a simple rod. Slightly cone shaped with the thinner end having the razer side on it. It wasn't clear until examined or rang like a bell that it was hollow and could make harmonic sounds. He pulled the cards from his bag with his left hand leaving the bag in the chair next to the pit.

Chapter Six: Knave of Coins

Henry Daniels enjoyed calling himself General; he was the type of arrogant sociopath that enjoyed being in charge. He was a misogynistic man on a warpath. None of the men under his control would see any of these traits at all until too late, except for his son David Daniels Jr better known as Junior with the men. He was named after his late and great war hero grandfather. He wasn't much different than his father other than his rank was considerably lower. The respect he got from the men was considerably nonexistent but Junior tried hard nonetheless. Spitting images of his old man in looks, personality and mannerisms yet he couldn't get the old man to acknowledge him or pay much attention to him. Unless that attention was abusive. Henry Daneils was an abusive father and person. This affected Junior mentally. He wasn't a mentally stable man as Henry Daniels knew this and used it to his advantage psychologically in trying to manipulate his son to do his bidding in war. He used psychology and fear to get a lot of men to do a lot of things in war that was General Henry Daniels MO. He tried to employ these tricks with women too, much to his dismay this backfired. Henry Daneils was a predatory man.

    The reality was Henry Daniels wasn't much of a general of anything. Really was more of a commander of a small ragtag Pride which is a part of a larger group known as the Men of Pride or the MOP. Henry Daniels was retired years before The Event. A forced retirement from the military for conduct with women under his command unbecoming of an officer. This was the point in his life where he started to crack around the edges and no one seemed to notice. Now he was taking a division of men north where they were going to try and stop the newly restored train tracks by blowing a big old hole in the middle of the system in eastern Iowa just west of the northern aggressors central base The Arsenal.

    His actual orders were to regroup with the larger forces on the eastern front and stop the train from its forward advance east from the Ohio side. General Daniels and the short sighted commanders of the MOP legions didn't see it the same way. Some orders were meant to be broken. America could not afford the mistakes of a few short sighted men. General Daniels was taking this war straight to the northern aggressors heart and ending it.

Travel was a slow, tedious and hard trek. America had changed very much; everything was rotting away, dark and trying to kill you. Most stuff was broken, destroyed, didn't work right or was in control by the enemy when you were in these territories. All of General Daniel's men were on high alert and most were road weary and tired from the traveling. General had 150 men with him, all of them dedicated to the destruction of the northern aggressors and the restoration of their American way of life.

They were a collection of various sized men from big and round to skinny and tall. They had all kinds of gear. Everyone was wearing a mix of camouflage and clothes. Some just had on camo pants and black shirts, others had full ghillie suits on. One man was covered in homemade body armor and carried a flamethrower that had seen better days. They walked at different speeds in a scattered row down the broken highway. Visible to all for miles. Most were talking loudly amongst each other. General Daniels was at the lead trying to estimate how far till they needed to find a camp to make base. It'd be the base of operations for this motley crew. They were within a few miles of the train site according to his map skills.

Junior was frustrated his gear had been chafing him for miles and his gun was jammed. Plus he needed a fix. He was hoping they would stop soon so he could fix the problems without anyone noticing they were bothering him. It was hard enough being the General's son but to be bad at it too was another thing altogether. He hated his father, the man was a jerk. But family was family and that was all you had these days. He said this to himself but he had left the responsibility of his children to his sick wife when he left to join this mission with his father. Juniors thought was broken when he saw a shadow moving quickly in peripheral vision. When he went to look he saw a shadow person quickly dart for the tree line. His heart leapt and he pointed his rifle at the trees, arms outstretched and shaking. He lowered his weapon. He quickly realized he was seeing things and the rifle was jammed anyway. His mind was back to its dark thoughts.

"The Northern Aggressors are trying to take your family away from you. They are cutting the south off completely with their central rail system. High Command knew what they were up to since long ago, that was how this war broke out. They want to take what is yours and leave you in the waste lands dead. They caused all this." is what Junior and many were told from so called superiors and in many different iterations. The ideas of why he was here when for the entire two weeks everyone was treating him like shit and beating on him. It was wearing him thin. He was extremely sleep deprived, all the men were. Junior had the added benefit of the effects of extended amphetamine use. He had been seeing shadow people for the last five days of their journey, Each day the shadow man was getting closer.

They started turning and jumping over the side rail off the highway. They were gonna break for a camp. Junior was relieved because it was a long day. It wasn't long before they found a clearing and men started breaking camp. General Daneils set men to the various tasks for making a fortified camp. He barked orders like a field general to beaten and broken men. They were all too tired and malnourished to put much effort into their actions. So the shabbling beginnings of a fort were under way. Junior was sitting on a rock in some ashen mud next to his pack trying to undo his jammed gun. He had come to the conclusion he needed to break it all down and clean it out. Easier said than done. He started laying out a cloth to work on in a secluded area of the group when a voice came from behind him.

"What the Hell do you think you are doing boy?" he could tell the voice belonged to his father, the General. He jumped to attention and turned to snap a salute best he could. "At ease, maggot. What the hell are you doing boy, you're not on break? Are you taking a freaking picnic? Pack your shit back up and hump your ass up to the highway. Isaac, Byran, Ben and Chris are going to meet you up there. You boys are headed to scout out the train tracks to see what we are up against. You are to listen to Isaac. You boys are to report back here to me within 24 hours. Isaac has all the details and knows what to do. understand? " General Daneils said this all while actually never looking at his son. He walked around his son imposingly, bumping him occasionally while walking circles around him with arms crossed behind his back and his chest puffed out.

"But Father it's...." Junior was met with the back of Henry Daneils right hand at full volume to his face. For as weak as Junior was, the frail old man was more so. For a full volume smack it barely registered with Junior.

"It's General!" Junior could hear the anger in his voice. Henry Daniels' old age left him a bitter man; he was once married with multiple kids, happily married and he was a retired ex-military living out his years in Texas training a young Pride of men before the event took it all away. He was a womanizer then. The women no longer desired him and when they did he couldn't even perform so he got abusive. He had even done so to his own son's wife. When she laughed at his shortcomings he beat her. Now he was stuck in the mud and shit with just Junior. Again, thanks to the Event. His hands were trembling and his head was shaking. It started to rain again. Junior started to pack what little things he had out without saying another word. He didn't look at his father, which was a mistake.

"I didn't say at ease, soldier." The steam could be heard boiling over in the Generals voice. "Get your head right boy or I'll do it for you." The venom dripping from the words wasn't lost on Junior. He launched a new series of blows to the back of his son's head. Left, right and left, right again. The general was coughing by the end of his triad against his only living son. Junior hadn't gotten up or even turned to look at his father till that cough. When he turned all he saw was the man's back as he stormed off into the darkness. The blows were superficial, they caused no real harm, the old man was weak and dying. The only reason he made up this suicide mission was he had the cough and was going to die. He just didn't want to admit it.

"I hope that cough kills you old man." Junior whispered to himself with the same amount of hatred in his voice that his father had. Junior looked up to the dark sky and the light falling rain. It sprinkled over his dirty worn face. He breathed deeply as looked into the sky for signs of how long til it was pitch black. Maybe a few hours. He swung his wet pack up over shoulders and clipped the straps tight. "I'll show him." He reached in his pocket and pulled out a bottle of pills. As he started through the camp towards the highway up the hill. A plan started to form in his head. From the treeline nearby a dark form black as the void of space, in the shape of man, watched intently. If it had facial features it would be smiling.

Junior was at the edge of the camp nearest the highway when he traded his pack for that of a supply pack full of explosives. The swap was rather easy as everyone was too tired to pay attention to anything they were doing. Junior walked slowly as he came to the munitions area. Johnny and a few men he barely knew were in the area unpacking their bags and what few crates they had brought. They had come with a few trucks that were packed with food and explosives. It was here these men were unpacking the explosives bags and food that Junior found his chance.

The few men tasked with this area of the camp had become distracted with the food stores when they got to the point of unpacking the trucks. The set of them had started to group together and discuss how to move forward with the process of unpacking the food supplies. An argument was well underway by the time Junior had figured his way over to the explosives and out of their sight. He didn't have enough time to unpack and fill his bag so instead he ditched his bag deep in the pile of explosive bags already piled up under a tarp and grabbed the biggest framed backpack in the pile he could find and threw it over his shoulders. It was nowhere near fitted to his size. But he didn't have time to fit it yet. He started to stride out of camp at a quick pace towards the highway they had left not even two hours ago.

The rain was only falling softly and with any hope it wouldn't get any harder. Junior was jumping the rail to get on the highway when he saw Isaac. "Hey Isaac, Are we gonna get any rack time I need to.." before Junior could even finish his question he was cut off.

"Stop right there you shit, you address me as sir. You will only speak when spoken too and there will be no special treatment for the General's little girl. Now shut up and fall in line." Isaac was grinning and the other men were laughing. Junior's face got red from the heat of his anger. He was gonna show them. The men had turned with Isaac and started the trek north. They were talking amongst themselves several yards ahead. Junior was exhausted and stressed. He had a plan now though and just had to keep holding on a little more. He reached into his pocket his stomach a twisted mess of knots suddenly. He grabbed the bottle of amphetamine salts and pulled it slowly so as to not rattle the bottle of pills. His eyes never leave the group of men in front of him. If he wasn't sleeping again then he was going to do it his way.

    He twisted open the bottle and took out several pills placing the cap back on and placing the bottle away. He threw the pills in his mouth and stomach instantly untwisted in relief of his needs. He grabbed is cantin and took a slug of water. He started to feel better, he knew he could show them all. The pack of old dynamite settled hard to the left on his back making him walk awkwardly. The framed pack had been set for someone of a taller stature. Junior tossed his shoulders in the reverse direction a couple times trying to get it to settle somewhat straight on his back. He did this while fiddling with his jammed rifle using both hands. Staggering back and forth in the darkness gridding his jaw. He was short at five foot four inches. His skinny frame was shaking as his body anticipated the surge of drugs in his system.

As night time began true darkness enveloped them. This area of the country was at the edge of the wastes. There was no electricity or people for miles. Junior stayed on course to follow the others by the sound of their voices. They were not exactly trying to be stealth. He had lost sight of them an hour or so ago. He lost track of time and distance due to the fact he was incredibly high at this point and had been messing with his gun while watching for the Shadowman. The shadow people had been following them closer and closer throughout the night. Which made getting the gun fixed all that more important. He was still fiddling with the bolt when he walked into the back of Ben. who was holding a map and talking with Isaac. Both had bright flash lights on.

"What the hell tinkerbell? Watch where you are going." Both Ben and Isaac stared hard at Junior while shining their flashlights in his eyes. Junior was holding an arm up to block the light.

"Sorry sir, Won't happen again" Junior cowered from the imposing men and walked past to find a spot to work on his gun he was going to need for his plan to work. It seemed they were set to take a break. The two men returned to their discussion and map gazing. Junior caught the flash of a shadow to his left and saw the Shadow man. This time the man didn't run. He couldn't make anything out. It was so dark and the figure was only several yards off but appeared as nothing more than a solid walking shadow. Blacker than the night. Then he was gone.

"I don't understand bro, we should have hit 80 and the area just north of the QCA by now. According to Daneils the base camp is set here." Ben pointed on the map to where they believed they had left the General and main group behind. We've been walking for almost five hours. Junior's ears perked up, five hours. Woah, something was way off then. They should have been in a position to spy the rails for morning light hours ago. "If we kept pace of four miles an hour that places us somewhere near here. We haven't seen a mile marker since Missouri, as I see it you have to choose Commander Isaac, One. We fire up our lights and find the nearest road marker or otherwise that we can use to locate ourselves on this map. Two we make camp for the night and move in the morning." Ben stood there while Isaac weighed the options. Isaac was enjoying the Commander title more than thinking. Really he wanted to sleep. They all did.

"Alright boys, here is how I see it. It's dark, and we are uselessly lost and tired. We are taking a 4 hour break. Get food, rest, water and whatever you need because after that we will finish the mission by finding the target zone, then we will need to head back to General Daniels with our findings. Am I clear?" a collective yes was heard from the men as they broke down collapsing to the ground in the piles. Two of the men were asleep within a minute. Junior sat there watching Isaac and Ben who were still looking over the map and talking. They were excitedly exchanging ideas as to where they could be. Junior smiled at those idiots and went back to tending to his jammed rifle.

After a while Isaac and Ben faded to sleep making all four men deep asleep. Junior got up and grabbed nothing but a small empty foraging sack and pistol then went off into the rotting forest area nearby. The world had been dark, wet and rotting long enough that fungi and mushrooms were taking over the seen world now. Mycelium has always been everywhere under the ground linking together across vast distances forming networks for the forests and nature to use and feed. This network also allows the Mycelium to consume the dead and rotting anywhere it turns up in the world and reintroduce its nutrients to nature. It starts the cycle of rebirth again.

Since the world was rotting, mycelium was there to consume it. This meant in order to survive you had to get along with fungi. The 1st thing was don't get the Black Cough. It was a death sentence, It didn't exist a decade ago. Since medicine has been taking baby steps backwards for decades now nothing has been found to aid in handling its symptoms or prognosis. The 2nd thing was mushroom identification. Knowing how and what mushrooms are was more a key to survival now then in any time in history, especially if you lived near or in the wastes.

Junior was quite adept at mushroom identification he learned out of necessity. It took him about an hour to find what he needed in the rotting wooded area. He did this always looking over his shoulder for the Shadow man. After returning to the area they had set to sleep at, he went to work. He started a fire and placed a camp stove over it with water to boil. He went to quick work cutting up the mushrooms he foraged from the area and placed them in the water to boil. He went to work searching through the other mens bags till he found a few MRE's. The meals ready to eat or MRE's were old military issues but some of them had real flavor, the kind that can hide mushrooms. Junior went to work making a meal for when everyone woke up.

Issac was first to wake up and was quick to wake the others. "What's all this, soldier?" he asked, trying not to sound either hungry or impressed. Technically it was dawn and it was starting to get a little lighter out. They still needed some aid seeing as making the fire a welcome early morning surprise. But a great smelling breakfast ready to go on top of it moreso. These men came to expect very little but punishment these days. To them this was a nice start to what would be a hard day.

"Making myself useful sir." Junior stood up at attention and almost dropped his bowl he was holding. Both the pose and the bowl were for show. He snapped a sorry salute with his right hand showing his nervousness.

"At ease, soldier. You did good." Isaac reassured him like a good commander as he started a stretch and yawn. Junior looked past him at Ben who was in similar fashion as he woke from his quick rest. Byran and Chris were brushing dirt off each other's backs as they made their way to the fire. Junior could hear them saying something about smelling awesome food. For a second Junior felt bad about what he was doing to these men. But he had to maintain his resolve this was for the greater good. His hand reached for the bottle of amphetamine salts in his pocket. He was going to need a big boost of energy to start the next stage of his plan.

"Come sit down guys, I made plenty for everyone." A touch of his eagerness showing. As he was watching Isaac gather a bowl from his gear he noticed movement to his left again. He slowly looked over. There just at the edge of the reach of the fires light was the Shadow man. Junior could see his featureless face. The Shadow man was shaking his head side to side.

Chapter Seven: Strength

"But it will cost a year of my life." Lex stated it with finality that should have ended the conversation about him summoning a demon right there. "It has nothing to do with am I comfortable with casting or calling down a circle to protect me this time Lady Rivers, it states in the summoning words, ONE CYCLE. I asked the Demon what that meant and he said to a human it meant one year of my life. A planetary rotation. And you're asking me to cast a circle, call one, make it dance and send it back. But it cost me a year. No." Lex tried flipping the Rod in his hand as it popped off his fingers and hit his foot slamming a small toe and bouncing out into the sandpit.

It slid a line through the near perfect circle Lex had drawn around himself minutes ago while casting a protection spell. It was his twelfth of the evening, complete with sigils in all four directions and all. And he was doing amazingly well as the High Priestess was testing them by throwing small projectiles at them to probe his skill. Several of the projectiles were tossed by some Imps who were slowly making ranks around the yard to watch the activities.

"Dr. Lex, I need you to trust me, I know it will. That being said you are not going to die anytime soon and not from anything those cards do. I know that much through divination. What I know is there are many powerful artifacts as well as other ways to extend your years on this planet. You may not have any or know of any of these yet but you will. And your worries of the cost of magick use and card summoning will disappear." Lady Rivers' eyes never left Lexs and she said this all with such conviction and power that he didn't just believe it, he knew it. A tiny Imp on her shoulder no more than a few inches tall named Krip, who was extremely playful broke out in enthusiastic applause. No one followed suit.

Lex had swiped up the rod from behind him from where it had slightly broken his circle. He held it close to his chest and breathed deeply. He closed his eyes and centered himself. He had decided to ride this trip out to the end. His left hand was in a jacket pocket finger brushing the width of the deck. Roughing the cards and making a sound Lex found southing. Bright witchlight fires burned with endless fuel in the bazaars around the pit. Many witchlights burned on various pole lamps and bazaars around the yard. Lady Rivers stood a few feet from the circle with Krip still sitting on her shoulder; he was tossing glowing witch lite balls in the air for his amusement. Her long flowing dress is tailing behind her. It's dagged cuffs flowing down her sides in the wind from her crossed arms. He pulled a card from the deck.

"Ronove." The name left his lips and carried on wind to the middle of the sand pit three feet from Lex's circle where it suddenly seemed to come from. Black and red smoke slowly started appearing and swirling in a vortex. It grew and grew in size as it formed parts of a hideous monster. Whose slimey icor dripping body came into view was massively top heavy with a disgusting mangled huge head. Its long gangling clawed hands were carrying a staff. Imps ran and hid. Some like Szuil stood by and watched. Krip covered his eyes and drove for Lady Rivers' bosom. Lightning crackled around the demon as he manifested.

"Summoner! Showing off your new toys?" The ancient voice of the demon was like nails on a chalkboard to the ears. "You're all going to burn." he swung his staff and knocked Lex right off his feet. Lex landed square on his shoulders. Throwing the rod, knocking him square in the back hard down, his head cracking the ground from the rebound. The blow sent lights through his brain and eyes. His sight and thoughts went askew in a bright flash. The demon took advantage of the broken circle.

"Lex! Banish him!" as Lady Rivers yelled this she threw her arms open wide. Her right dagged cuff moved frantically with action as her left arm threw a small bundle of herbs at the demon. She stepped into the pit muttering a spell. Her right cuff exploded with the head of a serpent that hit the sand and slithered to Lex who struggled to gain his senses nearby. The serpent was black as the cosmos with bright spots like stars throughout, it was as if the galaxy was moving past in the sand at incredible speed spaced like a serpent. It made a perfect circle around Lex. Etheric glowing runes dropped all around the snake from its body forming a protective circle. Right as the herb bundle exploded against Ronove's body in a cloud of purple smoke it engulfed the demon all for the ends of his limbs.

The demon Ronove had a hand full of the dazed and writhing Lex's hair. Ronove was pulling his head up to him at the very moment the circle from the cosmic serpent activated. The demon's hand was severed at that point in a spectacular flare of reddish light. Ajax broke from where he was seated and ran full speed for the circle. He reached the circle only to be met with its protective wall of stones. He could not enter the circle. He ran around the perimeter of the circle barking and growling. A group of Familiars grew in size behind him running the circle wanting to join in to fight the demon.

"Banish Him Lex! Lex banish him!" came the enchanted yells from the high Priestess Lady Rivers who was a foot off the sand pit floating on unseen energies in a glowing circle of signals that followed her movements. Inside the circle with her was Szuil and two other Imps brandishing weapons and enchanted amulets in their hands. Grim looks on their faces. The demon crawled at the smoke and shuffled around to no avail. Lex shook his head straight as he came to his senses. He remembered hearing Lady Rivers tell him to make him dance then send him back. Easy peasy, she said. Lex stood up.

"Rovone! Dance a Jig." Commanded Lex. All the commotion suddenly stopped. It was quiet. The Limbs of the demon Ronove started to flail differently in the purple smoke and he was stationary. The Demon was dancing. The demon started to say something But Lex cut him off. "Ronove you are never to speak unless spoken to. You will dance until told to do otherwise. And nothing else or I will uncreate Ronove." A whimper came from the cloud of smoke. Everyone looked at Lex. His hair was matted with blood as the demon busted old wounds open and caused a couple fresh ones. He was swaying back and forth slightly like a drunk person. "You know Lady Rivers, I can think of an easier way to show off battle Imps and Cosmic Snakes." Lex threw the jest at the High priestess as he collapsed to his knees and started petting the snake. He stared deeply into its galaxy like skin. It really did appear to have a universe underneath its scales. "What is his Name?

"His name is Orion, Lex are you ok?" asked Lady Rivers as she waved a flowing left hand at Ronove. The Purple cloud of Magical smoke blew away. The sight of the humiliated demon dancing endlessly and one handed amused her. It was the perfect lesson. Lex had failed and came back to win. Lady Rivers was able to display her powers and support Lex through the lesson. There was a lot more to work on though to get Lex where he needed to be.

"Amazing, I feel a year older and decade wiser." came the quip from the sore sounding Doctor.

"Lex I am sorry we should have tested your circle before the summoning, I …" Lex cut her off well before she could finish the self defeating thought.

"Lady Rivers, stop. That was the perfect test. And as terrible as it may of "went" I think we both know that was a great 1st lesson. I don't want to hear a word about you beating yourself up as a teacher. I'm not going to beat myself up as a student. So you're sure as hell not going to do it as a teacher. I dropped my rod and it broke the circle I actually saw happen. I don't know why it never occurred to me to redo it. You gave that speech, then Krip started applauding and I got all into it. So, It's Krip's fault. I blame Krip." Lady Rivers was passing the dancing demon and reaching a hand to help Lex get off his knees when he said the words. Krip came popping out between Lady Rivers' blouse . She was a modest Witch and did not have a very large exposed area of cleavage. So the Small Imp Struggled to get out. When he finally did get out he rolled in somersault fashion down her breasts. He launched himself like a cannonball yelling in a small voice.

"Bombs away!" he spun off the ends of her bosom, tightening himself into a round baseball size ball. "Weeeeee!" came his little attack cry from there as his launch velocity carried him towards Lex. He slammed right into Lex's chest with a little boom noise he made himself as well as a puff of sparkles and dust that Krip magically produced for effect. Lex was laughing in amazement at the creature as it ran off to grab the leg of Lady Rivers giggling and falling constantly on the way there.

"They are quite the sight to see in person aren't they?" Lex said as Lady Rivers helped him up. She lowered her right arm at the same time and Orion the Cosmic Serpent slithered back into his enchanted home somewhere in the High Priestess dagged sleeve. The circle around remained glowing brightly and followed her. Szuil was near the demon intently watching him. He had what appeared to be a custom pole arm in his hands. Its gold head glowed with a menacing threat of enchantment. Lex noticed the Imps full attire at this time for it seemed to have come to life in places now. Some details of the Imps clothes and jewelry now had glows or mild smoke like effects come off here and there. His belt was adored with little daggers and pouches. Even his two earrings in his left ear were cooling down from having glowed hot moments ago. Lex hadn't been kidding when he called them Battle Imps.

Ajax and the other familiars were sitting eagerly on the side of the stone circle having finished trying to enter. Lex waved to Ajax to relax and wait. "I'm ok Ajax, Good boy!" he yelled. The wolf rolled in excitement. So much so that he rolled over a black cat with a loud meow and a startled jump began an entirely new game of tag between the group of familiars. The demon watching the action of its tormenters from its position of dance in the sand could do or say nothing, just watch. Szuil and his friend Pairlut stood near the demon weapons drawn, eyes never leaving the ever dancing Ronove.

"Their Amazing, The Imps. Szuil and all of them. This whole world of magick . It's always been here. I feel I've known. So, what's it all just been hidden from mankind?" as Lex asked if he was watching the other battle Imp, Pairlut. He was the size of Szuil , about three and half feet in height and dressed in a fine tailored suit that had threads of empowering glow here and there. He had an assortment of straps and belts on him with various daggers and pouches on them. He had many earrings in both ears and a huge notch missing in one. He was missing his right eye as well. There was a huge scar down his face right through where the eye had been.

Instead of an eye patch he had a polished tigers eye gem formed into a glass eye. He was the most imposing Imp of the lot.

"No Lex. We've been in the open the whole time. Mankind chose not to see us. To not participate in this part of the world. Man decided many centuries ago to lean into the concrete jungle and away from the natural world and the spirit. They moved from magic and the world of the Faeries." The second she said the word faeries Pairlut and Szuil Turned rather heads with Pairlut talking in a firm and somewhat jestful voice

"Hey, that is a derogatory term, my Lady." Szuil shoulder pushed his old battle buddy. Some banter being exchanged between the two could be heard. Showing the depth and age of their friendship.

"Ofcourse, my apologies Pairlut." She said with a playful smile to the two Imps who were already looking at the demon again. She turned to Lex and they slowly walked towards the dancing demon. "The Imps are part of the world of the Fae the closest humans would come to understanding them is as faeries, but that word and its definition to humans over the years has lost all true meaning. People would think of Tinkerbell. And that is wrong. Do you know what a Djinn is Lex?" Lady Rivers and Lex were just behind the Imps now and watching the demon dance as they talked.

"Yes I do, But I have multiple meanings." he signed knowing he just made her point somehow.

"I bet you do, In the west we think I dream of Jeanie or Aladdin . The reality is that the actual Djinn are much different. They are entirely different in how they enact their tricks of magick . Fascinating race of beings the Djinn but not one you ever want to cross or make wishes with" The comment had him wanting to ask a million questions about Djinn. Before he could ever think of carrying that line of questioning she carried on. "Lex, we have a lot of training to do. We need to find out why Baal has brought these cards to you. Send this Demon back so we can talk in private. I'm sure you need to rest for tomorrow and the next few days as well" She turned and floated away towards the house. "Boys, clean up, I'll get the drinks. I think we all could use one."

This whole time Krip had been slowly and dramatically acting out a mountain climbing expedition up Lady Rivers body since he reached her legs. It was only now that Lex and Szuil had noticed as her back was turned and she was walking away. Krip was nearing her shoulders and acting out throwing roping and harnesses over all while managing his imaginary pickaxe. As he swung his fake struggle over the top he planted a fake flag on her shoulder and jumped up and down. He reached in his pocket and pulled out a little bag and threw it in the air. Lex and Szuil watched as tiny colorful fireworks exploded above the mini Imp and he jumped up and down enjoying them. Waving and smiling eagerly.

Lex turns to Szuil. "What is with the little dude?" laughing as said the words ``He seriously cracks me up." Lex waved his hand in the air "Be gone Ronvove, next we meet only dance till I speak otherwise." The last statement towards Ronove had a tone and finality that sent shivers down Szuils spine.

"Cracks you up?Are you ok? Lex?" Szuil said with concern for the doctor after the short display of darkness. Something Szuil hated to see in anyone, especially someone who would be near his mistress. Szuil's hands twisted on his polearm and it snapped to the size of a pencil. He sheathed it on his belt. Pairlut dual sabers were sheathed on his back safely as he walked away to tend to the Witchlight fires. "Where are the cracks, I can start a healing spell and I have some salves on me sir, Just show me.." he was patting Lex's legs and searching his body for cracks.

"Szuil, it was a figure of speech. I meant that he makes me laugh with all the little things he does. He is like a court jester." Lex was laughing and very touched by the concern the Imp showed for him. The Imp had known Lex for a matter of hours and was showing true concern for him. It was the sign of a good person and a true warrior Lex thought. "Szuil, Thank you." The Imp looked up at him and slightly cocked his head. It wasn't often if ever a human showed gratitude to an Imp. Szuil was a little shocked. Lex had only known Szuil a few hours and was already showing compassion and appreciation for him. Szuil understood this as a sign of a good man and strong witch.

Ajax barrelled into Lex as he exited the stone circle knocking him to the ground. The barrage of wet sloppy wolf kisses began in force. Several of them made their way up into the nose cavity of the doctor. Those felt like having your brain licked. Lex didn't mind so much. He understood the deeper connection of their bond now somewhat. Which left him with the feeling of empowerment he didn't have before. Infact this entire day has left him feeling more empowered and powerful than he has felt his entire life which was weird considering he walked around getting his ass kicked all day. He sat there petting his friend on the wet dirty dormant lawn watching the Imps tend to the yard. It Started to rain.

Chapter Eight: Death

Junior had a heck of a time grasping what he was seeing. The four unsuspecting other men ate and finished all of the food he had made for them in a short amount of time. He had boiled then strained a huge amount of poisonous mushrooms into the water he used to make their tang drinks and meal. They collapsed paralised within fifteen minutes of eating, none of them had even left the fire area. Junior had made his food separate and mostly it consisted of amthpedmine salts.

He was now standing there staring at the shadow man who had been following him for weeks. There he was plain as day at the edge of the fire. A solid being, whole and complete. Just a featureless void black being shaped like a bipedal man. He was even speaking to Junior. It was just that Junior was in complete shock that it was happening. He had been standing there for almost twenty mins staring at the shadow man.

"Hey Buddy, I'm gonna need you to snap out of it. I've been cool about slowly approaching you so you wouldn't freak out and you're still freaked out, my guy. Come on my dude. You and I are gonna do amazing things together my boy!" The shadow man waved an arm in front of him wide for effect and to break Junior's stare hopefully. He looked around at the four men on the ground. "Well shit, these guys screwed with the wrong umbrella. Did I say that right, buddy?" He looked up, at least his head went up. He had no eyes or facial features to indicate he actually was looking up, it just seemed that way. "Yea, No. Ombre. There it is." He seemed excited and got up from looking at the bodies and turned back to the frozen Junior "They screwed with the wrong Ombre!" The gusto in voice carried around the campfire and back to them.

He was standing in front of Junior again. Junior snapped out of it. "Who...What..I.." He stuttered and mumbled till he hit the ground on his knees. His hands were shaking and he started crying, his right hand driving for his pocket. Reaching for the familiar bottle and the rattle of comfort. He pulled them from his pocket to take more. Hands shaking violently he unscrewed the bottle. Suddenly the pills, lid and bottle all went flying into the mud. The intensity of a new round of balling and wailing starting as his incoherent speech came forth from the young Daneils mouth.

"Oh, hey buddy, do cry too much. Oh hey, feller it's ok you can take more of those. I like when you do that. It's ok they're gone. Here let me help you, my guy." The Shadow man got down on his knees in front of Junior and held his arm with his and with his other hand he waved in front of Junior's face. Like a magic trick he waved it twice in front of him and poof on the second wave a full bottle of one Junior's favorite types of pills appeared. The crying and sobbing slowed. The weight of juniors shoulders came to a calm more rhythmic flow. He wiped the stream of growing snot flowing from his nose. He started to try to compose himself at the site of his sin of choice.

"You did that for me?" Junior said with real emotion in his voice. No one ever gives him anything. Especially not one of his favorite things in the world. Most of all no one ever stopped and got down to comfort him. That's not what happened but that's how he saw it. "I thought you were here to take me to hell for what I just did" He started to get a little emotional again. He did just murder in cold blood four men he had know most of his life.

"Oh this stuff, ole chap." The Shadow man's head looked around. "I love this, this is awesome. I'm here to help you with more of this my dude" He hands Junior the bottle pills. "Don't worry my man, you're with old Mr. Frank now." The Shadow man lifted up off the ground easily taking Junior with him. He proceeded to brush the muddy ash and leaves off of junior to somewhat clean his outfit. "There we go chum, better than two mins ago. Now what do you say we pack up and go kill a witch my man?" The Black entity sounded very chipper.

"So Mr Frank is it?" Asked Junior, twisting open the bottle of pills. "What are you? Are you a demon or an angel? Did I lose my mind finally?" He popped another few pills. His second set since poisoning his fellow men. "I've been drugged out for a bit man. This could all be a hallucination or a dream. I mean what the hell dude?" He was starting to get fired up. The Shadow Man could tell. He wasn't ever really going to tell him anything if he didn't have to.

"Hey Pal I'm real as rain" lighting crashed across the sky in the background as a storm brewed. It started raining lightly. The entity's arms went out as he stood there in the rain but rainops never seemed to hit him. "You know what I am. I am a Shadow Person in the flesh baby. I am trying to become whole here. I just need a little help my man." he did a little spin at the end. "So check this out my guy. You help me and my boys become whole here in this world by simply killing one witch. Who works for your enemy. Then in return we will use all our excessive forces and powers to wipe out your enemies under your command my big bad warrior friend." He did a little bow for effect. He let the drug-addled mind of the messed up Junior do the rest of the math for him.

Junior thought hard. It was hard because he was incredibly high now. His mind raced at the possibilities of the outcomes of having a supernatural force win the war for him. He would be the legend of the south for all times. Conqueror of the Northern Aggessorers and Savior of the South. He never stopped to think how he would get there. The cost of the trip to that end. He didn't think about what this being truly was and what it was capable of doing. He didn't even stop to think if he was capable of even doing what was needed to achieve these ends. He just thought of being the Savior of the South. Crushing all beneath him and showing his father who the best was.

"Alright Mr. Frank, But 1st I have to see this train sight my dad had a hard on for." He turned to start rifling through the men's gear to pick out what he wanted and what he needed.

"Gee my dude, does the train sight have tits and ass?" Mr. Frank asked while he absorbed into his arm the entire explosive's pack. It completely disappeared. Junior missed the action of the pack absorption as he turned to Mr Frank in confusion.

"Tits and ass?" Then it dawned on him and he started laughing. "Cause the only thing he will chase is a skirt. Good one Mr. Frank. I think we are going to get along just fine." he continued giggling as he looked around. "Hey where the hell is the explosives pack I need to re pack things." Junior started to get frantic and shake. A normal person wouldn't have let panic set in so quickly but Junior was on a lot of drugs at this point and hanging out with an interdimensional being, so nerves were high.

"Hey now my Bro, Chill out. I got all the packs and gear my dude! Just watch." He bowed at the finish. He extended his void like arm and with the end the pack of explosives slid into view from within his arms and lay on the ground. "My dear friend I will carry many burdens for you on this journey of ours" The large framed pack of explosives was sucked like a speck of dirt into a vacuum right back into the arm of Mr. Franks within the blink of an eye. "Lets pack and go see these titties bro!" jested Mr Frank with much excitement for their partnership. He sucked up another backpack and a rifle up from the ground. Lighting struck the sky and lit up the night.

Junior and Mr. Frank walked towards the river side by side. They were taking a shortcut that Mr Frank decided on. Junior decided he would allow it. They were cutting through rotten woods and shrubs before long they came to overgrown mushrooms. The Mushrooms towered over the man and his extra dimensional companion. The smell was the most foul. Junior handed the machete back to the Shadow Person.

"What in the World?" Junior looked up and all around. This entire area as far as he could see was over taken and changed. It was a fairy ring. The largest fairy ring he had ever seen was made of sixty foot high mushrooms glowing with bioluminescence streaks.

"Oh yea. Pretty awesome my guy. I thought you would like this being a shroom dude and all." The Machete disappeared into Mr. Frank's body as he didn't even try to grab it from his friend; he just moved towards it and touched it. It was sucked right into his body.

"They're beautiful. Mr Frank? Where does all the stuff go when you suck it into your body?" Junior didn't take his eyes off his upward gaze of the mushrooms. He was in complete awe of them.

"Well think of it this way my boy, This body is like a space suit and I'm on the other side. When I take objects through I store them here like in a warehouse with me. Then when you want it I push it back through the space suit. Easy peasy my guy. Solid one second and void the next. my bro" As Mr. Frank said that he had his hands out in front of him and various items shot in and out of view through the tips of them to make his point.

"So you have a bunch of stuff in there? More than just what was in the packs?" Junior was asking because his mind was starting to think of the possibilities. Off in the not so far distance was the sound of heavy caliber gunfire.

"I do my inquisitive little friend but I think we are about to the bloodbath you wanted to see, we should take a peek then we really need to be off to kill the witch queen. Mr. Bill is waiting and we don't want to keep him that way for long." Mr Frank's head was moving around as if he was looking around behind them for something.

"Someone coming Mr Frank?" Asked a nervous Junior. "Who is Mr. Bill?"
They are moving a little more steadfast now. Mr Frank touched Junior's arm. His touch was that of cold steel. Junior slowly turned pitch black in color. "Hey what the hell?" he started to panic and wirth in Mr. Frank's grasp.

"Calm down Buddy, It's just a little camouflage look up, out of the forest towards where the gunfire is coming my guy." The calm matter in which Mr Frank said this eased Junior till he looked to the sky and made out the several large Harpies circling the air.

"Are those? Holy shit." Came the druggys response to seeing monsters in the real world. "Are they killing Northerners? those monsters?" Junior looked down, he was completely dark now like mr frank. "Is this?"

"Yes their Harpies my man, Yes they're killing your enemies so we don't need to go there and no the dark color is not permanent my dude so let's go kill their witch lady!" Mr Frank started to turn right and head away from the fighting direction.

"Mr Frank, can we please see the site like you said? Maybe watch a few deaths? Then go kill the witch. Please?" Junior put his hands up as if to ask pretty please.

"Oh my guy, anything for my witch slayer" The enthusiasm was electric in Mr Franks voice as he did an about face. They broke from the line of Mushroom Ring. They were unaware of the tiny little eyes watching them from the tops of the mushroom ring. There was not much cover, just low dead shrubs and rotten wood everywhere with fungus all around. Junior looked, they blended in well with all the dark color of decay from their black appearance.

They moved slowly around through the mess of brambles and dead brush. Eventually they came to the edge of the bluff they had been working towards and the location of all the commotion.

Chapter Nine: The Hanged Man

Gabe was feeling good. He had the humvee packed and the caravan ready to rock and roll with all the men set at Alpha Point in the East Village docking area tracks. Just no Lex, where the hell was brother at. Well nothing wasn't going to slow this down. "Cameron, Logan, Thomas and Leon. You are on point. Anton, Albert, Sam and Nikolas. You are all on rear guard. Reece, Romeo and Amber are with me. You know what to do, everyone stay frosty, let's roll out!" Captain Knight barked out the orders with charged vigor. The soldiers snapped a final salute and broke ranks to their vehicles while grabbing their gear on route.

These men and women were not a rag tag group, they were a well oiled machine. They all may not have worked together till today but they were all the product of years of military training and brotherhood. They knew exactly how to work together. Four of them have been with Captain Knight for years. The others, Military Command was able to transfer for this mission to fix the mishap at the bridge sight. Captain Gabe knew how to pick them. He was standing watching them break to make their positions in the caravan and take off. He made his way to the Humvee looking for Lex. A voice came from the point vehicle.

"On your call Captain!" Gabe was scanning the area one last time for his brother when he heard the call. He was disappointed Lex didn't make it. Then worry set in, he was forgetting something. He returned the call.

"Move out!" Gabe looked back towards the hill where their house was; he could barely see the road. It was morning and the clouds made it seem like night. He saw the flash barely, running fast like lightning low to the ground. Darting in a cross pattern streaking white as it came down the hill off in the distance. It was Ajax in brilliant form running to the caravan in a show of true effort that hopefully won't be lost on the troops. Captain Gabe was thinking if he should stop or make them catch all the way up. What if they were in trouble? Ajax was hauling ass.

"Amber, give me eyes." Gabe reached an arm towards her as he stuck his head out the now moving humvee. She handed him a beat up pair of binoculars. Their eyes met when they connected for the pass off. The moment seemed to stand still between them. There was an unspoken thing between them that they never seemed to have time for. Gabe looked away and used the binoculars to see how Ajax looked. He caught up to the running wolf after a few seconds frantically trying to connect. Ajax looked like he was smiling and completely happy. No distress or panic, just running to catch up with Gabe as if they were playing a long distance game of tag.

"What is it, Sir?" Amber asked with mild concern in her voice. "Should I halt the caravan sir?" she seemed more concerned with getting his attention the more he didn't want to answer. "Sir? Should I direct Romeo at any threats sir?" There were no threats he was scanning for his brother.

"No, It's Lex. His wolf is chasing us. I suspect he is trying to make it. They need to catch up" Gabe handed the binoculars back to Amber and looked forward as the humvees bounced along the round splashing water up bobbing along. He had a smug smile on his face. Amber pulled her red hair back tightly and frowned at the captain.

"Sir, may I speak freely." She banded her hair back in what she called a killing position. "We left roughly twenty five mins early per your command ,sir." She did her best not to break a smile. She had a standing friendly relationship with the Knight brothers and a budding romantic one with Caption Knight. At least she hoped the latter was true.

Before he even could turn to yell stop. The canvan came to a screeching stop. The three vehicles in perfect formation stopped with equal distance between each other. Each humvee slightly turned to make the gun on top as a line of sight to the man standing in the road. All three guns trained on the sole individual in the road. His long jacket flowing in the wind only parts of it stopped by his leather handbag. His long hair flows out in the wind from under his hat's wide brim. Lighting strikes the sky in the distance, lighting up behind. He held a duffle of steel tools in both hands.

"Stop messing around Lex! And get in the dam Humvee already!" The anger in Captain Gabes voice, more than apparent. Disappointing Lex even further. His brother had just left him behind while he got the supplies from the black smith shop for them.

"Forget something Captain?" Lex threw the duffle of tools into the back and jumped in. "You sent me to get the tools from the smith this morning dude? And then you're gone?" Lex leaned in real close to whisper this harshly to his brother. Ajax jumped in at that moment.

"Oh Ajax you smell great!" Amber said as she started petting the overly energetic wolfdog. Gabe responded to break from Lex's attack. Gabe had messed up. He knew it too. He backed out again, bad this time too.

"I gave him a bath last night. He was a dirty boy." he started petting Ajax too. Everyone and the wolf were packed in now. Gabe wasted no time and "move out" came the call

"Oh did you now?' Lex inquired of his brother's tall tale of bathing the dog. "Is that what you did last night?" Lex at that moment knew his brother's descent into full blown alcoholism was complete. Gabe however was blatantly lying to try to fill in lost time as well as make himself look good. He had no idea what he had been doing or where he had been up till quite recently. Other than black out drinking and having nightmares.

"Why yes, then I set up for today and got some rack time. What did you do?" Gabe painted a pretty picture compared to the horror filled night it really was. He remembered the nightmares but that was about it. He was thinking as hard and as fast as he could without looking like it. He stared back at his brother. He was being torn apart inside and yet all he could do was continue to destroy himself pointlessly. "Early night for the best of the best" a smug smile forced on his lips, his eyes giving away his lies.

"I got shit faced and passed out early. Thanks for telling me to go get your tools from the blacksmith this morning then leaving me." Lexingtons retort to his brother lies. Lex turned as he said that statement out loud and with intent. Reece, Amber and Gabe all knew what it meant. It was directed at the Captain and it was a statement of his behavior and actions lately. Lex, his brother, just called him out.

It got silent and awkward for a while in the bumpy ride. The dark terrain passed by as they drove by the enormous mass of the

Mississippi river which has nearly doubled in width in some areas. Much of the populated areas like the Arsenal had to put up walls to keep the water away. Some cities like Davenport just let the river eat parts of them up and moved the hearts of the cities elsewhere. Lex was deep in thought staring at the river when Captain Gabe spoke to him.

"How'd you do that? On the road back there?" Lex could tell from his voice that he was impressed.

"Magick." Came Lex's quip to brother who left both him and Ajax standing in the wind.

"Dude Shut up. You didn't magically appear in front of the lead jeep dude. How'd you beat us?" Gabe was visibly uncomfortable as he was adjusting himself in his seat and constantly looking at the front seat to see Amber. None of this was lost on Lex.

"I was down the hill in front of you at the black smith in the east village getting your tools. I saw the caravan leaving so I ran towards the river going north. I didn't think I'd ever make it. But Cameron spotted me from the lead vehicle." Came the smooth even response from Lex. No one in the ride was paying them any attention so Lex decided to press some conversation. "What have you been doing really brother?"

"What do you mean, Lex? Been busy with this mission, you know that." He was straight up ignoring eye contact with Lex now. Lex knew he was going to start pulling away. "Where have you been? I've needed you, you know?" he jumped too fast at saying this. He felt he was being attacked and started to go on a kind of defense. He was digging a bigger hole for himself.

"Gabe, I've been looking for you at every turn when you're off work the last two weeks.. You're either in the only bar drinking or home passed out drunk. Both of those very much involve avoiding me. In two weeks you managed to make plans with me and not show up or send me somewhere then not follow through on your end a total of six times. I've been researching caves on this mission, I've found out much about the cards. I met an old friend of Mothers, whom I tried to get you to go to meet with me. I've cleaned the house and the dog after you the last few days and this morning I ran to get your tools while you ditched me yet again. I've been trying to be your brother. Where have you been?" Lex stared concernedly at this sibling, head bobbing with the movement of the road.

"Don't give me that shit Lex. I don't have time for it. Sit back. I'm busy running a mission." Gabe's face was bright red and hot with fresh anger. He was acting mad at Lex but really he was just angry that he was being called out for who was truly being lately. He looked around for something to do. He pushed his radio to his mouth. "Cameron, how are we looking brother? Over." Veins in his face were popping out all over as blood pulsed through his head. Lex looked out the window toward the north. It was slowly getting lighter out, lighter for this day and age. He started some breathing exercises.

"Dark and clear. 20 min. Over" Came the quick crackling response from the lead humvee. It was silent and tense for the rest of the ride. Ajax started whining and trying to move in the back as they approached the site. Lex turned back to tend to the dog.

"Ajax buddy what is wrong boy?" He started petting the dog when the humvee was hit and rocked hard from the top right a loud screeching howl came from the sky above. Romeo was in the gunner position and wasted no time firing. Lex had never been so close to live gun fire of such caliber. He jumped into a huddle position in his jump seat grabbing his ears and squishing his face. The comms went mad with chatter and gunfire erupted everywhere. Ajax crawled at the back door and howled to be released. Lex heard the sound of doors pop open.

"Who has eyes?" Captain Knight was yelling as loud as he could over the gunfire. Everyone was shooting in the air. He scanned for their target. He found it as it came back in for another dive on the middle Humvee right towards Romeo. It looked like a disfigured condor. It had a wingspan of three meters or more. It was a monster. Its screech was loud and echoed in the valley. Most of its features were darkened at this distance so it was hard to make out but this poor bird was tortured and mutilated. The hail of bullets seem to hurt it every little. With frightening speed it closed the gap of space and they all saw it in full glory.

The Harpy was a full human woman in size. Naked with feathers covering most of her body she had a long jagged and broken break instead of a mouth. Her arms where long ragged wings ended in clawed hands. She had muscular legs with large oversized clawed fowl feet. Bullets howled, blood splashed her body and feathers everywhere. Her constant wails pierced the air.

Their awe cost them. She nailed Romeo head on through his fifty cal gun fire. She took a mortal wound in the action. Clawed feet ripped into his chest and shoulders gripping him. She tore him into the sky and carried him off with her. Romeo screamed in agony and writhed the whole time. Blood sprayed from the entry wounds of his chest. His screams died in the wind shortly after. The Harpry twisted and turned higher into the sky. Receiving bullets to its body the whole time. Bleeding from a gaping wound Romeo dealt her before being carried off.

"Kill It! Kill it, Dam it!" Captain Gabe had rolled out of the way unnecessarily when the harpy hit Romeo. Better safe than sorry. He continued to drain his magazine into the beast screaming to kill it. Fog of war enveloped them all. They didn't understand what they were fighting, just that they needed to win. "On Me, On Me!" Gabe shouted as he moved out from the vehicle's cover. Four of the men followed as they shot the beast in the air. They were making for a better angle of fire as the beast moved away from them. It worked, the beast was taking massive fire. It was done, it reached the zenith of its flight and came crashing back to earth dead.

It crashed between the five men and the caravan. The horrific sound and scene it left behind made more than one of the men puke. Cameron said he puked because Albert did but no one believed him. The blood ran everywhere and mangled limbs were intertwined. Ajax had pushed his way out of the humvee and through a door finally. He was running towards the scene barking. He was clearly upset and started doing circles again. Captain Gabe acknowledged him and his early warning.

"Thanks for that heads up Buddy, sorry we didn't understand your early warning." Captain Gabe went to pet him. Gabe heard the sound of the train horn way off in the distance. The engineers were gearing up to head here. They needed to make sure this place was clear. Ajax was still spinning.

"He is still warning you! Look out there is more coming!" Lex yelled as loud as he could as he tried to get out of the door as smoothly as possible. His hand bag caught on something and he tripped, it released and he fell out the door into the mud on the ground. "Look out!" The two soldiers remaining in their gunner nests turned their guns on the sky west of their position where Lex indicated. The expression on their faces told Captain Gabe all he needed before he even turned to look.

"Fire at will!" Left the Captain's lip at full volume as he started turning his head. To his horror high in the sky above the bluff was several more of these hard to kill bastards just circling like massive vulchers. As soon as the hail of fifty caliber gun fire started to reign upon them their screeching started to permeate the air. Then the dive bombing began. "Take cover!" Captain Gabe looked for where to direct his people to go. West was the cliffs and newly blown out caves with lots of rubble and hiding. But lots of unknown and most likely where these monsters came from. Possibly what they're protecting. North is nothing, it is all open as he continues to scan.

A loud crash bang came from the rear jeep as it was knocked askew from a harpy ramming into them while sliding to its death in the mud behind and to the left of the vehicle. The gunner blew the harpies' face off during the process of it bombing. Captain Gabe stopped to check the battle. Amber pulled a RPG out of the back of the middle Humvee and crouched in the ashend mud. Lighting started to stroke the sky in a series of crashes around the background as a storm brewed. Rain started to come down lightly. She aimed the RPG with intent. Captain Gabe watched with admiration. His heart ached as he watched water wash down the side of her face. She remained calm in the chaos around her.

A brilliant flash of light blared out from behind her lighting up the area in bright orange red. The rocket propelled grenade hurrelled out the front on a steady stream of fire. It looked to be on a wild frenzied path bound for random destruction. It went several dozen yards upward into its target's cheek where it exploded in a radiant show of the spectrum of light fire produced upon combustion. It tore through the harpy leaving nothing but a set of twisted legs with bulbous bleeding meat attached to them falling to the ground. Part of the blast knocked another harpy off its flight and into a nosedive. While a third had the blast mangle its wing beyond flight capabilities.

"Amazing ." Whispered Captain Gabe to himself. Gabe Looked a little to the right of her and saw Lex struggling to get up. He was yelling something that Gabe couldn't hear. "Sargent! Grab Doctor Lex! Everyone, let's move for better cover! On me." Captain Gabe hadn't finished scanning, he knew the newly blown out caves were possibly bad. He also knew to trust his Brotherly instinct. That instinct was screaming to trust Lex. Now he hadn't heard Lex yet. He didn't need to. It was clear on his face. He was looking up to the west. There were too many. They needed to run for cover from the sky. Caves were the only cover here.

Suddenly three of them hit the lead Jeep with screams and twisted metal that knocked it into a series of flips. It rolled end over end till stopped over the other side of the train tracks on its side with the undercarriage facing the men. Cameron was a gunner in the jeep. A long time friend and teammate of Gabes.

"No Cameron!" The man ran hauling what they had with them shooting as they went. Providing coving fire for each other in sequence. Ajax ran past everyone quietly and stealth; he slipped through the maze of rubble and made his way to the mouth of the cave entrance that the early engineers had made accidentally. He was so quiet no one noticed him. "Dam it. Do we have coms with Command?" Captain Gabe's voice was steady and reassured the men that he was calm and in command of things. They started to tighten ranks on him. "Let's make it to the mouth of the cave." Lex pulled his rod from its sheath on his back and checked to make sure the cards were close at hand in his pocket.

"No coms sir. We need the Jeep radio sir." The expression on Reece's face as he reported the news was concern for he didn't want to be the one to run out there. They sat in silence for what felt like eternity. A hard look came over the Captain's face as he thought.

"Well if we don't call then the train full of privates and engineers with guns and supplies are coming up here anyways. If we do call and say we need help, who are they going to send? Those boys are already ready to come here. They are trained, armed and can fight." They hustled in couched positions amid rubble and large boulders as they talked it out.

"No one is getting to the vehicles alive." Lex chimed in and pointed to the sky between them and the jeep. Several Harpies had turned into dozens circling the area. They were fighting amongst themselves here and there. Occasionally one would even be killed from the foray and fall to a crimson explosion of gore below. Where its kin would promptly eat its corpse. They had been concerned with plans while Lex had been watchin the Harpy horror show unfold.

"Jesus Christ Captain what the Hell is going on?" The soldier's voice was shaky and he was pointing his gun upward.

"Logan I wish I knew." replied Captain Gabe. "Ok team, let's find a defensive point till the cavalry gets here." Gabe's eye caught Amber and Lex who were staring wide-eyed at the cave. Gabe Looked over and into the cave entrance. Ajax came running out at full speed, completely silent. The cave had a luminous warmth glowing in it. There was light coming from the depth of the cave. Lex started for the large open sand and mud area in front of the cave mere yards from them. "Lex! Wait, what are you doing?" Gabe's stomach dropped into his legs watching his brother run towards the unknown, then Lex stopped in the clear area suddenly and started drawing in the ground. His stomach changed emotions as his brotherly entanglement changed gears. "Alright people, On Lex! Cover him but stay clear of his work! Do not shoot unless engaged. We need to stay unknown as long as possible." then he whispered to himself for reassurance. "I hope you know what you're about to do brother."

On the ridge above in the dank rotten brush and broken trees lay unmoving two dark figures. If anyone below had the time to sit and look long enough they would eventually spot the silhouettes of the impossibly dark people. One turned to the other.

"See Buddy you got better places to be my guy. I'm telling you, friend. Those people have bigger weaknesses down river. I can show you. You can really hurt them. You can't do any more damage here than is already being done. Hello, my guy. Let dad come finish the stupid tracks and you go take the prize. Blow their witch queen up. Come on buddy, Mr Bill is gonna do something drastic if we don't get moving my man." The other dark body lay there watching.

Chapter Ten: The Devil

Lightning streaked across the sky, its thunder crash came a few seconds later. Isaac lay unable to move in the mud. Dirty thick water was starting to pool inside his mouth as he slid further down into the ground. His mind was struggling to process information and think clearly. What had happened? Who was that dark man Junior was talking to? His vision came and went like his ability to think.

"So I bet you flesh puppets don't want to die from mushroom poisoning?" Came a nice smooth sounding disembodied voice. "I could help you not die there in the mud, say for a favor?" The solid black silhouette of a man in a trench coat with a long brimmed hat came into his view somewhat. The man knelt down so Isaac could better see him. Although he was still solid black very were like a walking shadow and his face was featureless. "Cat got your tongue? Oh so you want to die? There in the mud" The man got up to leave.

Isaac eyes wide in horror as he was trying with all his heart to scream "Please no help me!" He screamed in his head but he couldn't force the words to come to his lips. No way could he, he was paralised. The Hatman suddenly turned back around and sat on his heels again. With an inhuman speed and with no mouth to speak from, he said.

"I'm just kidding Isaac. I'm gonna help you and you're gonna help me." The Hatman reached out and touched Isaacs arm on the skin. His steel cold touch froze Issac to the bone. Almost instantly Isaac started feeling better. Isaac started moving, as he felt something draining from his body. He started stretching in the mud on the ground. He spit all the mud out of his mouth. It turned into a cough which escalated into vomiting. The Hatman patted his back.

"How do you know my name?" Isaac coughed out. "Where did they go? Did you see where they went?" Issac was gaining energy and his wits fast. His mouth tasted of the fowlest rot. "Did the General send you? What is going on.." He started getting panic in his voice as he looked over the Hatman more and more trying to rub his eyes and blink his vision better. He was getting antsy and moving away from the Hatman. Lightning flashed again showing the featureless intense blackness that was the Shadow person. The Shadow man looked like a solid void black person, pure black as space only unlike Mr Frank this one had a long brimmed hat and coat to appearance.

"Slow down kid, I'm going to heal Ben, Then you two will go get David Daneils Jr and Mr Frank and put them back on course. I'll heal your other two buddies here and get them to go get General Henry Daniels to bring the group up here to fight the northerners that are over there under the bluff. Agreed?" The Hatman had a hand up like there was no way to argue this. Isaac didn't care this guy wasn't incharge he was and he was gonna show him.

"Look here." Issac got a grim look on his face and pushed his finger in the Hatmans chest when he did this ripples went out like he had hit water and then his finger froze to the hatman chest. A surge of the poison came back on him and he felt the paralysis coming back on in a rush. He looked the hatman in the face. Where his eyes should be two red orbs glowed. He spoke in a deep piercing tone from his otherwise featureless face.

"A favor not to die in the mud. What is it gonna be, flesh puppet?" The red eyes burned through Issac and the poison was almost to the point he would collapse.

"A favor!" he yelled as the Hatman released him and he fell to his knees in the mud. The glowing red where his eyes should have been was gone. "What do you need me to do?" Issac sounded almost broken. A fresh round of vomiting came from him. He sat there on his hands and knees retching in the mud.

"Are you gonna piss me off? Were you not listening to what I said?" The Hatman was hard to read visually due to his lack of a face and was a literal walking shadow. But his voice gave way all of his short tempered anger and annoyance towards the questions coming from the soldier. He appeared to be acting like he was smoking a cigarette or something, but there was no actual cigarette. " I just said I'll heal Ben and you two go get David and Mr. Frank back on course while the other two of these flesh puppets go get the general and the pride to help fight the other flesh sacks that are already there." Hatman was leaning over and crouching down. He started the process of healing Ben of the poison. Ben looked dead. He was lifeless face down in the mud. Issac stood there staring at the only friend he ever knew. It just occurred to him what David had attempted to do to him here. Rage filled Issac.

"Yes sir." Issac got up and stood at attention while moving his head around to scan for his stuff. Everything was gone but their eating utensils and the fire they made. Junior somehow was able to take everything. He was gonna kill that weasel for the humiliation he caused Isaac. Issac stopped to look at the weird Hatman who had his back turned to him. He was black as the void of space.

"You are still messed up from the shroom's, try not to overthink things Issac, I'm just here to help. You can call me Mr Bill" Ben was trying to stretch and wake up but he was having trouble. "Help your friend here while I heal Chris and Byran. As soon as you two can move, haul ass that way." he pointed off towards a broken tree line away from the road they were taken.

"Don't ask me anything Issac, just look at the ground over there. They left a very obvious trail of footsteps and broken stuff, what do you call it….shrubbery. Mr. Frank made sure there was a trail to follow. Move fast. Issac, just get them back on course. You don't want to die in the mud." Mr Bill was hunched over Issacs companions messing with their limbs. He dropped one of Chris's arm's in the mud. "Tisk Tisk" He shook his head

"The Bloody Hell!" Ben was quick and had discovered their new friend's strange appearance as well as their unusual situation. He was scrambling in the mud to back away but gaining no traction as he was backwards on his ass and with Issac trying to help him up. "Issac what the hell is going on, sir" he scrambled for a sidearm that wasn't there.

"Just calm down, soldier. Mr Bill is here to help, We were poisoned. You are still under the effects. We need to move if we are to catch Junior and make him pay." The two friends caught eyes and a shared hatred crossed their faces.

"Ah evil eye, good. Go get them back on course, Understand? Mr Frank is there to help. I'll be there with the Pride shortly." Mr Bill never even turned to look their way, just kept fiddling with the body of their now dead friend Chris. Only Hatman knew he was dead; the men weren't really paying attention. The two of them returned knowing looks. They weren't listening to this guy, whoever he was, it didn't matter if the general did send him to help. Junior was a dead man when they caught up to him.

"Yes Sir!" With that Issac helped Ben up onto his feet. "Junior stole everything or got rid of it, so we have to get creative. Are you ready for this?" They clasped hands tightly and yelled "Ho ya!" in unison. They turned and broke into a full sprint off to the trail that Junior and Mr. Frank formed earlier.

Mr Bill paced around the two bodies and kicked Bryan hard in the side. A release of air could be heard. Mr Bill scratched the side of his face. A figure approached him in the somewhat lighting up morning from his left side. This figure was also pitch blach in appearance, almost a carbon copy of Mr Frank. Mr Bill didn't move, just stood there arms crossed staring at the dying man.

"Hello Mr. Alan, So good to see your suit is fixed. Feel like wearing a flesh puppet?" There was a change in Mr Bill's voice, he sounded genuinely happy to see Mr Alan. More so than it sounded when he was talking to the human men just moments ago. I have a feeling we won't be walking into The Men of Whatever Camp looking like Shadow People." Mr. Bill was tapping his right foot. "There's a little less than hundred and fifty men there with the leader in the dead center. I think flesh puppets are the only option." He sounded like he was trying to convince Mr Alan. Who he turned to as he finished talking. Mr Alan had just settled for a standing position next to Mr Bill. He kicked Bryan's body hard. A release of air came from the lungs of the dying pridesman.

"Well Mr. Bill, this one is still alive. Really flesh puppets? Again? It never works" Mr Alan was walking around the other side of the dying man. Mr Bill turned and moved towards the body of Chris and turned him over. There was a loud sucking sound in the mud "It worked in Frisco." He said matter of factly. Mr Alan grabbed a stick and started poking the body of Byran.

"Don't call it Frisco. I would like to point out that I just got this suit fixed." He hunched down on the balls of his heels. "Should have taken Mr. Frank's job, again. Really wish we could help this guy die." He cocked his head to the side looking done at the man. " I mean I could turn him over, But then he might live longer. I can't force his face in the mud." His head cocked side to side as he observed the paralysed man.

Mr Bill grabbed the chest of Chris and proceeded to shove his right arm into Chriss' like he was putting on a shirt. He turned to Mr Alan while brushing down the brim of his hat which disappeared into the side of his head. "You know the rules Mr Alan, you can only help them kill themselves and others..." his voice trailed off while he shimmied his head up into Chriss skull like he was putting a hoodie on. He continued to get into his Chris suit like it was a jumpsuit or one piece of clothing. While discussing things with his colleague. "They have so many organs."

"It's gross, They are gross. Why are we doing flesh puppets? You're already half-dressed and mine is still alive." Mr Alan was shaking his head back and forth now. "Can't we flip this kid over and revive him. give him a chance to take us to the general. He is alive. He should have died. They are gonna think we are zombies or something and shoot us. Hundred and fifty stoned ass hillbillies see dead compatriots come walking back, no gear, dead eyes, motionless faces. Saying don't shoot it's us, only their lips don't move? It's Mexico City all over again. Only it's not a bet this time." He kicked Byran again, only not as hard as he had been doing. This time Byran jerked away from the impact and wheezed out a noise with his release of air this time. The Shadow People both suddenly jerked their heads towards the body and cocked them to the side with peaked interest.

"You should be dead already." Said Mr Bill in a frustrated voice to the now shivering man in the mud.

"You really shouldn't be able to move either" added Mr Alan excited at the possibility of not wearing a flesh suit. The man's shivers were ever so slight but it was apparent that the mushroom poison did not have the lethal effect it was supposed to have when it came to Byran. "Mr. Bill, Heal the man so we convince him to save the south please. He is the savior of the south." Mr Alan went right into a routine. He started straight for Byran in the mud and grabbed his arms, rolling him fully over in his lap. "He survived the poison of the traitor...shit what's your name?" Mr Alan started snapping his fingers at Mr Bill.

"His name is Byran. It's not gonna work. He can't hear you do this act Mr Alan. That human is dead." Mr Bill was adjusting the hips of his human suit. He was a grisly sight to look upon. The organs and internal parts of Chris could not be absorbed like the poison or packs and guns had been so them as well as the bones and other unneeded tissues fell out the the "pant legs" and "cuffs." What could fall or get pushed out Mr Bill "helped along". The skin and clothes were left on the shadow man like a poorly tailored stained suit. The man started to vomit and dry heave in Mr Alan's arms with gusto. Mr Alan did all he could to assist.

"I'm here now, sir. Get it out. Mr Alan is here to assist. Mr Bill will have you fixed up in no time." There was silence for a while Mr Bill continued to adjust his suit and think. He finally came over and placed a shadow dark hand on Bryan and removed the poison from him.

"There we go sir, I bet you can feel the energy I'm giving you filling you up now, I'm here for you Sir." Added Mr Alan. The Shadow people looked at each other. Mr Alan was good at making things up. He wasn't doing anything. Mr. Bill simply removed the poison. The energy boost the man felt was normal. If he believed Mr Alan then this might actually work. If he didn't it still may end up being fun for the supernatural beings.

Byran went from shivering to constrinting his limbs. His jaw flexed up and down and ended in clicking sounds. He called out in agony as he regained control of his mind and body. Lightning screamed through the morning sky bringing its boom of thunder seconds after it. The pitch black shadow people hunched over Byran urging him to live again.

"That's right, leave the light and return to the damned." Mr Alan rubbed and soothed the man physically. Bryan's head was bobbing like a slinky trying to get a fix on either of the two dark fuzzy figures aiding him to health. He continued blinking and staring confused at the shadow people. Unable to fully grasp what was happening.

"Who...who are you.." Byran's voice trailed off as he struggled to talk. "Did I die?" Byran was blinking his eyes and his heads was moving erratically around trying to get a bead on Mr. Alan's face. He looked at what had become of Chris and how Mr Bill was wearing him. He started vomiting again. When he was finished shortly after he looked up to Mr Alan's featureless face. "Are you Death?" his eyes were watering up.

"I don't mind if you cry Sir. But, No. I am not Death. I am Mr Alan. At your service and this is…." he started for Mr. Bill but was waved away by him from completely doing so. He continued on another way as Mr Alan was very adept at weaving storylines for humans. "..your second chance at life Sir. Sir Mr. David Daniels Jr has done a terrible thing. He must be stopped. You have been chosen to fix what has been put into motion by him and evil forces. I'm here to help you on this higher calling Sir." Mr Alan would've carried on had Byran not tried to force his way up and out of his embrace. He started in with comments and questions effectively cutting off Mr Alan.

"Wha...what are you?" Byran's voice trailed off again. He was still struggling to see which was a good thing for the shadow people. "Where are we?" Wait. Where is Junior? I Thought I heard Iassc talking with Ben." Byran shuffled around and stumbled on a rock. Mr Alan caught him.

"Slow down Sir. All in time." We need to get you proper medical attention back at camp. Sit down for a rest then in a few moments we need to get moving, sir."

Mr Bill had walked off into the background to shred his flesh puppet. It was working out as the arm had now ripped and fallen down in a flap over his hand. A hand he was using to hold up the leg to his hip ripped as well. He was moving quickly and silently as he did not want to notify the others. They were quite too busy with bryans recovery to take heed. Mr Bill slipped behind some bushes and shed all of the suit off himself while the organs and bones left a trail showing the way he went.

"Never works!" Mr. Alan yelled from beyond the bushes. Mr Bill chuckled to himself. His faux hat brim popping into place launching gore off into a shrub.

"Why did you yell that? Asked bryan looking confused at Mr Alan. He was starting to cry again.

"Oh Sir please cry, But it has nothing to do with you, A friend Mr Bill. is all Sir. I promise." replied Mr Alan in a sweet and sincere voice. "Tell me when you think you are ready to make the walk to the camp Sir." It started to rain again.

Chapter Eleven: The Star

Junior sat there watching with delight from above as the men below him scrambled from the onslaught of harpy attacks. He was even laughing at the chaotic scene. Mr Frank on the other hand was taking turns watching behind them and below.

"Hey my guy you saw, we need to move down the river to find this witch or Mr Bill is gonna do something drastic here bud." There was urgency in Mr Frank's interdimensional sounding voice.

"Dynamite." Came the cold even response from David Daniels Jr.

Below between the new cave openings, mass of spread out rubble and the tracks was a clearing of even flat sand. In it was a small group of people one of them was frantically drawing a circle with a metal rod. Lex made the circle as wide as he could to give them space. He tried as hard as he could to stay focused on the words and intention of the spell he was casting as he drew the circle of protection around his friends. The group was standing tight, back to back shooting their rifles into the air covering Lex and each other as best they could from the occasional charge of a circling harpy.

"Lex! Whatever is in the tunnel is almost here brother!" Captain Gabe yelled to Lex over the constant ring of bullet spray. A Harpy slammed into the ground in front of him yards away it started clawing its way in the sand towards Gabe screaming in the process. Gabe looked in the eye, reached for his belt and pulled a hand grenade from it. "Fire in the hole!" he belted as he tossed it right in the front of the mutant bird woman's path. She slid her broken body over it as she continued trying to tear her way to Gabe through the sand. "Bye Bitch." Captain smiled at her as the explosion rocked the beach and blew the front half of the monster to smithereens. Blood and eversine came showering down on the group.

Right as the rain of blood settled to the ground Lex had come full circle around the group. He continued to move around the circle to the four cardinal points of north, south, east and west where he etched weird symbols in the sand. He was speaking under his tongue so Gabe couldn't make out his words as he watched his brother perform this strange ritual. As he finished each symbol he would step back and with outstretched arms look upward. With this motion the symbol began to glow purple. Gabe's eyes wide with amazement. He had seen and heard his brother talk of and do magical things but it was incredible. If Gabe wasn't so impressed he would have noticed that everyone had stopped what they were doing and were now watching the doctor's amazing ritual.

"Everyone in the circle quick!" Yelled a frantic Lex, who unknown to him had soft purple glowing eyes. "Whatever you do, do not break the circle! Do not leave the circle!" Everyone was standing or almost fully standing in the circle as he finished saying this. All of the wild eyed looks on their faces now in full view for Lex. The Purple glowing of eyes fading fast. "As long as we don't leave the circle we are safe." Lex was visibly exhausted from the ritual of making the circle.

"This is gonna do what, sir?" Right as the question came from Logan a Harpy slammed into an invisible wall the circle produced upon contact from the harpy as it tried to assault the group. A glow of purple with sparks flared out from the point of contact. The bird woman screamed in distress. She slammed back into the sandy mud. All of the Soldiers turned their weapons on the mutant and opened fire point blank into its head and chest. Her torso was reduced to a hunk of twisted meat in a minute as they drained the clips into her.

"Strictly badass." was the 1st thing Thomas had said all day. He was loading a fresh clip. "I'm getting low on ammo, sir. Lex you got a ritual for that."

The other soldiers started laughing and chiming. "Holy shit man, are you a sorcerer?"

"This is the end of the world isn't it?" came another

"Witch."

"We are…." The last one got cut off by an increasingly impatient Captain knight.

"We are in the shit people. Get it together. Lex is a dam witch. A Good one. Like Gilda. So snap out of it cause the only reason we are alive and may continue to do so is him. Now let's make sure we get him and us home. Am I clear?" Everyone locked their attention on their captain, all chaos around them ceased. They were beaten up, covered in mud, blood and guts. Ajax was spinning in place, barking at the cave mouth again.

"What the actual heck? Sir. Look!" Leon was pointing his rifle at the cave and it now had a brilliant white light that illuminated the entire area: sky, beach, tracks, river and all. Floating in air in the middle of the cave was a car-sized ball of vivid smokeless fire, a ball of plasma. Turning and swirling in and around upon itself.

On the bluff above Junior was opening a pack of explosives when the light aided his sight. He stopped to see what had become so intense it lit all that was there. Mr Frank chimed in instantly.

"It's time to go my guy, that thing right there. My dude. That is, what can I compare that to?……It's a demi-god.. We need to leave now, friend" He grabbed for Junior who stared at the magnificent flameless fire ball.

"That thing is alive?" He was holding a bundle of TNT sticks with a long fuse in one hand. "Can you light this Mr Frank." As he was speaking Mr Frank was reaching over to suck up the pack of explosives into his arm for safe carrying. With one hand Mr. Frank grabbed Junior's arm. With the other he expanded three knife hilts out the end of a balled fist from within his body magically. Forcing Junior to look at him.

"Of Course my guy, take a knife. You wasted too much time. Mr Bill is pissed. Soooo...." Junior gave him a confused look and grabbed the biggest looking handle drawing out an eight inch blade into his free hand. While he did this Mr Frank released Juniors arm with this action the pure black appearance junior had for camouflage disappeared. Mr Frank then lit the fuse while finishing his statement.

"....Now this is gonna happen." Mr Frank backed up several steps. Pointing with both his arms behind Junior.

The train could be heard making its approach. It wouldn't be long before help was here. They should see and hear trouble long before they arrive. It was a train engine with just a few cars of men and supplies. It would provide firepower, cover and the transportation they needed out of here. All they had to do was hold on a little longer thought Gabe. Through the screeching and gunfire came a holler. Gabe turned towards the tracks. In the twisted metal of the lead Jeep some arms popped up and pulled a head through.

"Captain! I called it in. They are coming in hot! HOOAH!" Cameron pulled himself from the wreckage. He reached back and pulled a bag of something up as well as a Beretta pistol. He stood up and steadied himself. "HOOAH!" He started letting loose with a Bereta as he slung the hand bag over his shoulder. He reached in the hand bag with his free hand rummaging through it. He pulled out a hand grenade.

"Cameron! Run! Get over here!" Captain Gabe went to leave the circle and go after his stray soldier. Amber grabbed him and held him back in the circle.

"Captain, no you can't! Sir! Don't!" She dropped her firearm to the sand. He struggled to be released from her grip. The train horn was heard in this moment cutting through the sounds of the warzone like butter. It was slowing its momentum as it approached the area but that would do Cameron no good as the wrecked jeep he stood on was sitting half on the tracks. Captain Gabe was feeling like he was the only one aware of this. He pushed to be released. These would be the last horrifying images the Captain would see.

"Cameron the train!" Screamed the Captain in complete terror as the events unfolded.

The harpy came to dive at full speed for Cameron. He was aware of the train over the rifle fire. He leaped up and backwards as the bird neared its final approach to grab him. His legs falling in air level with his eyes as he chucked the hand grenade in a wobbled arc towards the position he was in previously. The Harpy missed its target and crawled on twisted metal. The frustrated monster's jagged beak snapped out towards where the man was going, grabbing at the object he had tossed. The whole time accepting the soldiers gunfire like it was a nerf gun. Cawing in defiance of the weak assault. The bird creature raised its wings and headed upwards to take off right as the train hit it and the jeep in an explosion of fire, metal, and gore. The grenade had exploded. The train carried through coming to a stop shortly after in a screeching of brakes, sparks and fire.

During all of this on the ridge above junior had turned to see what Mr Frank was pointing at behind him. His eyes went wide with shock and dread. His hands started shaking. He dropped the lit TNT bundle to the ground and it rolled close to the edge. He started to drop the knife but quickly fumbled it back to grips with both hands. The whole time mumbling. "What the? You're dead! I killed you!" he stammered and tried to reason. "Mr Frank, why?" He didn't have time to look over his shoulder at Mr. Frank but if he was able he would have found that Mr Frank was nowhere in sight.

"You little shit. I'm gonna kill you junior " The venom was dripping from Issacs voice. He was a sight to see, covered in mud, pale white and rushing at Junior straight on down the bluff. Malice in his piercing blue, almost white eyes, foam and spit coming from his mouth as he clawed dead shrubs from his path like a wild animal. He had nothing with him. It looked as if he intended to kill Junior with his bare hands.

"I...I...I Did what I had to. You deserved it. you bastards....always beating on me!" Junior Steeled himself enough to stand up for his actions for once. It was enough to make Mr Frank who was sitting out of sight in the bushes, say something that would save Junior from death.

"Hey my guy, look behind you." Came the disembodied call to Junior's aid. Junior for some reason instinctively turned a full one eighty around with added momentum to move forward pushing off his right foot hard. It was like hitting a brick wall. He was so preoccupied with Issac he never heard Ben creeping up to subdue him from behind. His body scrunched up into him with the full force of his weight. Pushing both his hands and all eight inches of the knife up and into the chest of Ben.

There was a warm splash of blood over Junior's hands as the knife slammed into the man's stomach in an upwards motion from there it easily pierced its way up into the chest cavity. Slicing lung and heart in twine. Ben was so surprised by the move it barely registered at all with him. He had no time to comprehend that he had ended. He looked past what was happening to him. He locked eyes with Issac. It looked as if Junior pushed his body from the bluff. In reality he was pushing away from what he had done.

"Noooooo!" Screamed a heart broken Issac from yards away on bluff. Mr Frank watched in amusement as he noticed both men were crying over the death of Ben.

"Psst. Hey my dude…..might want to face Isaac. He is pissed" You could hear the laughter in Mr Frank's voice. He sounded like a kid at a birthday party. Junior turned his head towards Issac. He didn't know where Mr Frank's voice was coming from but he figured he would be able to hear him.

"Why is this happening Mr Frank?" Junior was sobbing as he fumbled for the dynamite. Issac was almost on him. Junior sat there on his knees wiping snot from his face with one hand and he got a grip on the TNT with another. The lit fuse almost burned down to its end. "Tell Mr. Bill, we can kill the witch now. I got to see the river. I just wanted to see water." He whipped the TNT at Issac who was a few feet away now. Issac yelled something incomprehensible and batted the bundle away. It spun over the bluff in an arch downwards. It fell several feet before it exploded.

The blast was immense limestone rock and fire blew forth from the bluff in a magnificent outburst. Below the mass of smokeless fire, the plasma ball came into action at the events above. A burst of energy was sent out from it in a wave of destruction. Rocks and metal in the radius of the wave melted or were thrown for meters while melting. The circle of men stayed safe all for the leg and arm of one Captain Gabe Knight who was struggling to get to

Cameron before the train hit him. The wave melted the limbs to nothing. The circle of magick around the team stopped the wave of destruction from melting them. In the process it cauterized the limbs closed. The force of the blast reverberated in the circles' magick walls like a large ringing bell. It was so loud and hard the force knocked everyone of them unconscious.

The Harpies had turned their full attention to the train the second its horn was heard wailing nearby. The team on the train had received a call from Private Cameron of the situation unfolding at the bluff. The men on this train were ready. It was a heavily modified train. As these were modified times. It had a couple gunners nest and a twin missile and fifty caliber system on one of its cars. The train was AI controlled; it was simply maintained by a conductor.

"Full Stop!" A call from the train. Soldiers poured out and into defensive positions around the train. They looked up to see what had been knocking the train.

The Conductor inside stepped out only to have a harpy grab him by the shoulder in a spray of blood. Soldiers were pouring out and taking defensive positions around the train. They had taken stock of the situation already unlike the conductor. They began to open fire on everything not human.

"Hel…" came the only half intelligible word from his mouth as the bird lifted him off. Then came a familiar man from the middle car of the seven car train. He seemed to float off the train car more than jump. It was Major Lightfoot in full military garb looking majestic as ever. Barking orders to men with precision and results the military expects. He slowly walked to the front of the train. Chaos reigned around him as he took in the field of battle and results of the explosions. He laughed.

"Johnson, your team is to recover Delta from the beach head they established. Collins, your squad will cover Johnson and his men, Everyone else covering fire." Major Lightfoot pointed to the crater with the large rock pile behind it. In the middle stood a landing with a group of soldiers all piled in the mud and gore together. Total destruction around them rocks, ash, fire, smoke and dust all settling from the multiple blasts in the area. No one questioned anything they moved into action. Harpies dove and attacked everywhere. Mens screams and gun fire was picking up all around them as the battle intensified. One lone harpy fell dead in front of the Major. He looked at it sideways. "Well hello my little friend. A Harpy, I haven't seen this trick in centuries. Who would do such a thing.." his voice trailed off as he looked up at the circling army of Harpies and then over to the now resealed cave and destroyed area of the bluff.

A Harpy received several shots to its leg forcing it to release the conductor from its grip. He fell to the ground on the other side of the train from where he started his journey. He landed with a loud cracking thud. His moaning came out more as a wheeze as he had a punctured lung and was quickly bleeding out from multiple wounds. Some of them were from friendly fire. He turned his head slightly to the right as he heard someone talk.

"Sorry brother" The young wild eyed man looking at him held a pistol in his hands and pointed it at the conductor. A hand bag slung over his other shoulder and a grenade in his other hand. The conductor recognized him as the man on the jeep that they couldn't avoid hitting with the train. "I can put you out of pain?" Cameron looked hurt to even be asking. The conductor could tell he held the resolve to do it.

"No. Please, The train. We saw you too late…Trainwreck" his voice was hard to hear as it was hard for him to speak in his last dying moments. He struggled to speak but needed to pass his torch to this young man. He if any. "Take this key…it…is for…the train….you are the conductor now….." he was taking a chain off his neck as he tried to hand it to Cameron his hand went limp and he died. It fell to the wet muddy ground. Cameron picked it up in confusion and wiped the mud from it.

"What the what?" he whispered to himself. He shook himself back to the now as he heard the Major's voice on the other side of the train. He made a mad dash around for the other side.

Major Lightfoot stared hard at the bluff and its lower caved in area. "What happened here? And who lives there, pray tell?" He asked himself. He turned to see a young man desperately running towards him from around the front of the train. A familiar young lad.

Cameron was winded and trying to speak. He was doubled over heaving with a pistol in one hand and a grenade in his other. He stood straight up with his mouth, removed the pin to a grenade and tossed it high into the air. A harpy swooped in and grabbed it up. Cameron snapped a salute with his now free right hand.

"Private Cameron Sir, Delta Team, I have this key from the Conductor sir." He flitched with a wide smile on his face as the explosion above them showered blood, gore and then dropped a hunk of monster meat down nearby them in the mud. "I'm sorry to inform you sir he did not make it." Cameron held the key out for the Major to take. The Major stood there staring at the young smirking Private. Blood streaked down his face.

"Do they go after anything in the air you throw?" asked the major. Visibly impressed with the Private's little show. "At ease, hold on to that key…….Conductor. You're getting a field promotion son . Get on that main engine car and plug the key in. Get this train ready to move out on my call. " Cameron was at ease but snapped a salute with the key in hand. He tossed a grenade high and far to left over the train. He was confused about certain parts of his orders but understood the whole. He turned away yelling 'Hooah!' somehow in unison with the Major as a harpy exploded in a fireball of carnage to left over the train.

Chapter Twelve: Knights of Cups

Lady Rivers was sitting with her favorite Imps watching the familiars wrestling in the dormant grass of the yard around the training pits. The morning dew was building especially fast in a basketball size spot next to her on the ground as compared to the rest of the yard. She was laughing deep in her belly at the familiars playing in the yard. There were several cats trying to catch Lavi, a large size bobcat in a game of tag. The popping sound was barely audible when the mushroom popped from the overly damp spot next to Lady Rivers chair. The mushroom grew and grew. Towering Its way up and till its mushroom head was formed a perfect domed shape next to the arm of Lady Rivers.

It was a gorgeous mushroom. Brilliant red with yellow orange spots that swirled their way back into the red. Its long glistening stem was of a soft hue of yellow. Lady Rivers took no notice of it as she sat there enjoying the foloricing of the familiars. Pairlut, a battle-hard Imp companion of hers was tending to the fire pit nearby. He turned to ask about the day's activities when he noticed the tell tale calling card of the mushroom.

"My Lady, if you would. I believe The Mycelium Throne is calling." The Imp smiled as he pointed to her left at the colorful mushroom. A look of concerned interest came over his face. It wasn't every day a Fae court calls.

"Oh my dear Pairlut I believe you are right." The high priestess looked from the Imp to the mushroom and back to the Imp again. "Well I won't keep the King's Court waiting. How do I look?" She brushed her hair around jokingly with hands.

"Stunning my Lady." The Imp Smiled and almost even laughed a little. The High Priestess took her left hand and placed it on the mushroom firmly. It seemed to sink in a little bit. There was a glowing yellow light around the edges of her hand. Her body went rigid and she snapped back into a straight position. Lady rivers eyes went wild as her pupils went wide and the color seemed to disappear. Her eyes rolled back into her head. Pairlut looked at The high priestess then he looked around the yard. No one seemed to notice what was going on. He sat down on the earth to watch his mistress. If there was any sign of distress he would sever the connection to The Mycelium Throne with one slash of a saber to the mushroom her hand sat on.

Lady Rivers meanwhile was on a journey in her mind through a connection to the mycelium network. She was off to visit the court of The Mycelium Throne. It was a Fae Court, Mushroom Fae to be exact. Better known as Faeries to Humans. This Fae Throne was currently held by the Grand King Bolete. He was a just and kind Fae. He was also a friend to the High Priestess Lady Rivers.

Lady Rivers was riding a pipeline of bluish white light. As she looked up it was black darkness everywhere except for the immense networks of interconnected pipelines of different colors streaming in all directions. They went to and fro at varying speeds and distances before breaking the unseen surface above her. She was underground in the actual mycelium network experiencing it on a spiritual level. The pipeline moved at exceptional speeds but held no danger to the High Priestess as it whizzed her along its route. The sight of the network was amazing. She knew the pipelines to be the mycelium. She also knew the different hues of light within them to represent the many nutrients and carbon being moved from trees and plants around. The mycelium was helping care for the world.

Her trip through the majestic world ended when the pipeline softly landed her in a circular area with one throne and several seats nearby, as well as some stadium seats around the side. It was lit up in the throne room with bioluminescence from the mycelium and some extra help from some will o'wisp floating around the chamber. It was mostly empty except for one Fae Mushroom Knight in full armor standing there looking mighty standing at attention.

The Fae's helmet was shaped like a mushroom cap with the skull of a Fae painted on it in white. The brim before the dome of the Helmet was a razor all the way around and the dome itself has various lengths of spikes dotted throughout it, dripping with a highly viscous liquid. The armor shone every little as it was a flat charcoal color and made of the finest Fae metal. The paladins were adorned with viciously long spikes that were visually stickly with poison. This adornment of spikes and poison continued down the Fae's armored arms to their elbows which ended in log outward curved edges dripping ever so slowly with the toxic goo. Their lower half had the same grim features. Flat charcoal color armor with imposing spikes from the long impaling kind on their knees to their toes all dripping with a viscous toxin.

    The Fae bowed curtly at the arrival of Lady Rivers. They held a dangerous looking halberd in their right hand. The toxin never seemed to drip off them anywhere. The Fae removed their helmet. The halberd stayed standing magically in the position where they left it. Their long hair came out with a shake of the head. It became apparent to Lady Rivers it was not a male Fae.

The Fae held the helmet at her hip. Her face was gorgeous. She had sharp features and beautiful silver hair. She spoke in a voice so kind it betrayed her demeanor.

    "Welcome High Priestess Lady River. I am Death Cap. King Bolete is away from this area of the Kingdom. Sage Aseroe Rubra of his most trusted counsel has sent me to give you information your highness. I am sorry for any intrusion and disappointment this may have brought to you my Lady." The Mushroom Knight bowed again.

    Lady Rivers was most impressed with Death Cap.

"Lady Death Cap how could I be disappointed when I get to meet such a Fae as yourself. May I shake your hand? It is a custom in my world." Really Lady River wanted to get a closer look at this most impressive of Fae warriors. "Your armor and its defensive toxin is quite the sight to take in. I have not seen the King in many years. I take it the news is not so terrible?" They were standing a foot apart now. They shook hands while Lady Rivers fully took in the Fae.

"It is not good, My Lady, Sage Aseroe Rubra and some Fae have been building Fairy Rings along the Mississippi river as you are aware. One of the rings, The ring above Orla's Run, north of River Manor location, was crossed by Shadow People who are working directly hand in hand with humans not friendly to your people." It was a mouthful to say. Death Cap stared at Lady Rivers.

"Orla's Run you say?" Lady Rivers' mind was working as she took in the information. The Fae continued her story.

"That's not all a battle has broken out on the ridge since they crossed. The Humans exposed a cave system in the bluff of Orla's Run the weeks before. Now today after the Shadow People crossed again there were multiple explosions. Humans are fighting each other, The manifestations of Harpies and the Shadow people as well. My Lady, Orla, has come to the surface and blasted the exposed cave opening closed. The Harpies are most likely her magical creation.

The Shadow People are going to bring more humans to that area within the next couple days." The Fae was going to continue but Lady River didn't need or want her to feel like she even had to. It wasn't the Fae's battle and they had already done more than enough for the humans here. She put a friendly hand on the Death Cap's and smiled warmly at her.

"My Dear Lady Death Cap, I will take care of Orla and bring her to a safe place before she kills all of North America. Tell Lady Aseroe Rubra My deepest thanks. The Fae of The Mycelium Throne have always had River Manors back and the Human species back as well. Is there any way we can thank you?" The question was rhetorical what could an old witch really do for something as old and all powerful as the Fae.

"There is one last thing then My Lady. Sage Aseroe Rubra said to tell you Misty Pebbles is around, she is looking for the Saum boys." The Mushroom Knight looked somewhat confused. "She said to mention it was The Sidhe who told Misty they were here." Finishing the statement and only adding to her confused look. She ended by placing her skull painted mushroom helmet back on.

"Misty Pebbles you say? Ok. Please give her my thanks and well wishes." Lady Rivers was starting to look inward at the last few bits of the conversation before turning back to Lady Death Cap. "Wait Lady Death Cap. Thank you so much for your time and effort to do this, I really appreciate it. It was a pleasure to meet such a fine

Mushroom Knight. I hope we meet again under better circumstances." As the Lady turned back the way she came one of the pipelines reached down from the roof and she sat sideways on it and was whisked off to her body and home. Off through the mycelium network of the world.

Pairlut was sitting there with his right hand on his cheek and his left eye on his High Priestess Lady Rivers. He was sitting criss-cross applesauce awaiting her return. He was watching her in case any sign came that he needed to cut the connection to the Mycelium throne from here. A scenario that has never come up when communicating through the network. He began to breathe in deeply when he saw the tell tale sign she was returning.

Lady Rivers' left hand was sitting on the trippy looking mushroom when the light around it came to a more enhanced glow and started shaking ever so slightly. Lady Rivers' body began to shake a little bit in its rigid position before her head snapped forward. Her eyes rolled forward and undilated. She shook her head to get her senses back.

"Oh Mama!" came her first words as she blinked to regain her vision. "That is a trip every time." She started coughing. Pairlut jumped up to his High priestesses attention. He stood in front of her. Hands on her knees.

"Are you okay my Lady? That cough." he was overly concerned and showing it.

"Oh my dear Pairut, I'm okay. Just some stuff in my throat from leaning back. I don't have the dreaded cough. My dear, did you sit guard over me the whole time? You are such a sweetheart" Pairlut was blushing. It was just hard to see in his grayish purple skin. "Pairlut, Things are a little worse than we thought, we need to come up with a pretty solid plan if we are to help all of our friends. Old and new. We are going to have some unwanted visitors close to our home. They have Shadow people with them." Her face was twisted in a frown by the time she finished informing her dear friend. "Where is Szuil, we have some tough choices to make."

At that moment Lavi the bobcat came barreling around the corner with several feline compatriots giving chase. They whirled in a frenzy of feline fur streaks. Walking up behind them with a precarious load of wood in his arms was Szuil. He was cursing in Impish as the clowder of feline familiars had almost knocked him on his ass and the pile of wood everywhere. Lady Rivers and Pairlut found amusement in the situation. They were sitting and giggling at the old Imp together.

"Szuil, we need you to come here." The High Priestess asked in her kind voice. "It's been brought to my attention that the problems of the world. Frankly our problems have gotten incredibly worse in the last half of a day." Her voice was a steady stream of kindness. Szuil Looked from around the pile of wood he held as it blocked his view of her. He peaked around the side and he glanced at her but really took in stock of the area around her and the mannerism of her. It took no more than a second to see the now dying away mushroom used for communicating with the court of The Mycelium Throne. Something that hasn't been needed in years. He could have dropped the wood. Instead with a powerful heave he tossed it as far as he could towards the middle fire pit circle. It landed mere feet away from the dying fire in the middle of the sand circle.

"The Fae called on ye, My Lady." His voice was solem. "How was the old King Bolete?"
Szuil face gave way to the fact that he was making small talk as he walked over to his friends to find out the truth of what was going on. Pairlut chimed in to get the conversation going for everyone. He wasn't one to beat around the bush like these two.

"Shadow People. Szuil, your favorite." The Battle Imps exchanged grim looks. They had more than a few skirmishes with the shadow people in their day.

"Lady Rivers, may I go on sabbatical?" Jokes Szuil as he pulled an enchanted dagger from his belt. He admired it in his hand twisting back and forth. It appeared to magically vibrate at an extremely high frequency.

"Oh Szuil, I know you don't mean that, I'm happy to see you still have my gift I got you from the last time we encountered The Hatman and his thugs." She looked to Pairlut for some type of confirmation he had the required weapons to fight such monsters. A weapon she had gifted each of them before the last time they had to face such evil. Pairlut tapped on his hip belt twice. The lady nodded as she was impressed. The Imps had many weapons they collected over the centuries of their lives. They could choose to keep any number of them on hand or in their pocket dimension homes. Pairlut's home item being an earring and Szuil's home item being a ring. Both items the Lady always wore.

"The Fae informed me that Orla's cave system was breached. She has been woken up and surfaced during a battle between the two sides of Humans, Shadow people, and Harpies. I'm assuming one side of those humans is ours and Lex is with them and the other is that of the MOP. Orla sealed the exposed caves with a blast. It's most likely the Harpies are a manifestation of her powers. It seems the two sides will retreat. But that being said the Shadow people are coming back with the rest of the MOP army in a few days to Orlas Run per the Fae. We need to prepare Lex to go back and get Orla safely back here to us. Before they provoke her into destroying the entire northern hemisphere." She knew the last part would bring the objections.

"Bring her back here!" One Imp yelled

"Destroy the northern Hemisphere!" the other Imp piped in.

"WEEEEEEE!" Out jumped Krip from one of Lady Rivers hip pockets. He ran down her lap as she sat there at her knee. He took a big jump and put his hands up in the air. He had one of her handkerchiefs. He made it into a parachute as he slowly wafed to the ground screaming "weeee!" the whole time.

"So when you're all done throwing fits at me or running away. I need help with a plan." Came the concerned voice of their high priestess as she sat back in her chair. She pulled something from the dagged sleeve of one of her cuffs; it was a packet of herbs and some papers. She started to roll her wrap of herbs to smoke. Pairlut smiled wide at the action.

"My lady, would you please roll me one too?" he inquired for the first time in decades. Szuil looked at his friend and then Lady Rivers.

"Please my Lady, we can split it." He caught glances with Pairlut and they nodded at each other.

"Of course my dears . Since you decided to calm down I don't see why not." She didn't look at the Imps as she was busy rolling her mind altering herbs. One would stop and think now isn't the time to do drugs. These weren't those types of drugs. The Imps were sheepishly looking away embarrassed at their little outbursts. Krip had landed and was rolling around in the dormant grass throwing dead grass blades in the air as he went. Not a care in the world.

They sat for more than several moments together smoking their herbs in the morning air. Thinking about their ordeal, rather everyone's ordeal. The familiars were still hard at trying to catch

Lavi the Bobcat in their never ending game of tag around River Manor. The Coven was fairly active with life outdoors this day. Something that had been very seldom occurring since the Event. Many of the Covens witches have been away off and on for the majority of the years since the Event happened. The world was in need of their help. It left Lady River with the duties of watching the Manor and it inhabits. This was not a very difficult task as the Imps could do this on their own. Especially in these times where human life was low on the planet and centered on things other than coming by the Manor. Much time passed as they smoked and then came the words.

"Seal of Solomon." Came the sad voice of Pairlut.

"We can't do that to Reginald! Besides, what are the chances Lex hasn't lain with a woman in 2 fortnight?" Szuil's voice was high and he stood up tall in a fevered rebellion to the idea of even thinking of using Reginald. Lady River slowly and intently stood up. Her face was stern and the Imps both knew she had resolved herself to a plan.

"My friends, the situation is dire. Probably more than we want to admit. Reginald is getting old. He is meant exactly for a situation like this. Pairlut is right. If Dr. Lexington has been abstinent, then the timing is right. The days are right. The ritual could be performed and for 24 hours we would have the Seal of Solomon for the Doctor to use to defeat the enemy and get Orla out without the need for too much bloodshed or Orla going nuclear."

She was really appealing to Szuil more than Pairlut as Pairlut had come up with the idea. She stood arms folded in front of her Imp friends. "We won't do it without asking for Reginald's blessing." she added.

"Lex would be able to get close enough to give a message to Orla that would stop her from destroying the northern hemisphere." Szuil said this while staring blankly into the air in front of him. He had been caring for Reginald his whole life. "What if the Doctor is...you know?" the Imp shrugged his shoulders like it might have happened.

"I may have lied to Lex a little when I said he doesn't die for a long time, Szuil. But he certainly isn't dead yet." She smiled at the sly Imp. "Now go to the rooster and let's visit with him. Pairlut? will you please get some other Imps together and start preparing for the rituals all out of sight of the 1st pit area, please. Maybe we can put up a partition for our friend. We will use the 1st pit area to have a celebration for Reginald should he agree." The good mistress knew the black rooster would agree. It was a matter of Lex being sin free. It started to rain.

Chapter Thirteen: The Chariot

Lex's ringing ears didn't seem to hold him back from trying to get up. It was the bodies piled on him. There were a few of them. Slowly the weight was shifting at 1st then it started to move quickly.

"Sir! We need to move!" Came the only voice he heard in what was forever. Lex was trying to figure out where he was and what was going on. When it came flooding back he jumped as high as he could but a body was on him still. The voices of yelling soldiers and screeching harpies came into focus as did his vision. A soldier reached a hand for him as the man on top of him was lifted off and carried away. Lex couldn't see much further than the man's hand but he knew what was dive bombing behind him.

"Is he okay? Are they all ok? Where is Captain Knight?" The onslaught of questions were expected by the young Sergeant helping Lex up.

"Sir, I need you to breathe easy, Everyone you had in this defensive beach head is accounted for and safe. We got Captain Gabriel and a few of his men to the train safely. Now we have to get the rest of you there. I am Sergeant Coleman. We are here to help Sir." He stopped talking for a second. He looked back towards the train. 'I'm afraid I will need to ask you to assist me in helping us make the train Sir. Do you mind fighting with us?" The soldier knew he was asking Lex to die next to him in an attempt to run the gauntlet to the train.

"Holy shit!" The words left Lex's lips as he saw what the Captain was asking. Lex took in the carnage. "How did you get them to the train alive?" The scene was havoc. There was nothing but bloodshed for the Harpies and the Army soldiers. The ground was littered with carcasses. Soldiers were around the train firing from all angles. A few men fired from around Lex and Sergeant Coleman's position. Lex noticed that every man from here to the train was on the ground in pieces. The 1st group made it because the Harpies hadn't noticed them, after that they knew. Now they were just waiting for them to run it.

"Everyone in this glowing circle now." came the strict order from the civilian Lex. Sergeant Coleman looked at him sideways, he was also defeated and said without second guessing it.

"On the Doctor, people! You heard the man! Move it!" His voice cut the chaos and those few remaining men of his plus the three remaining from the group that came with Lex made sure they were in the still functioning magick circle. Lex pulled the cards from inside his jacket pocket and started to rifle through them. As he was filing through them he came to the Baal card. It was moving and talking.

"Stop. Dr. Knight. What are you doing? Don't call a demon here in front of those men. I am here you fool. I am right in front of that train with your brother who is badly injured. Now I can make you all invisible and no one will know. You can just walk off the beach slowly. Tell them you're tricking the Harpy eyesight and make sure no one shoots any shots or their dead. Got it?" All three of Baal's heads seemed to be talking at once so there was a croaking and meowing at the same time.

"1st what do you mean badly injured is he gonna be okay Baal?" It was obvious Lex wasn't doing anything else without a clear answer.

"My Dear Doctor, he will live a full life. He lost a leg and an arm. He wasn't fully in your circle when the blast happened. I am making sure he gets the finest care." Baal was more serious and even toned then Lex had ever seen him be.

"2nd you're here? In front of people?" Lex seemed surprised and concerned at the idea of Baal being in the public eye.

"I told you I was high up in the military, I also told you The Knight brothers are important to me. Are we really going to do this right now?" Baal left the question hanging there till a harpys scream followed by its explosion broke the silence.

"3rd why aren't we invisible yet?" Lex quipped at the demon.

"You still have to ask. It costs a cycle." The demon seemed to be jesting back. Only it did cost the doctor a year off his life.

"Of course it does. Baal just do it." Lex was tearing up for his brother Gabe. The card melted only to be reconstituted back into the deck after the wish was completed. The team was invisible to their enemies, as long as they didn't attack them. That would give away the invisible person's position. No one had noticed but the Harpies were attacking only when attacked upon.

"Everyone, walk slowly. Do not look anywhere but forward. Do not shoot your gun or attack with any weapon. We will trick the harpies if we don't attack and move slowly. Just watch me do it 1st if you don't believe me." Lex picked his words carefully so as to be clear. He also tried to keep his voice as steady as he could. He was upset that his brother was messed up badly. His voice was a reflection of that, not a reflection of his belief in crossing this gauntlet alive.

No one followed Lex at first; they let him walk slowly and alone more than half to the train before anyone decided to attempt the insane walk he was doing. None were under the notion that they were invisible to the enemy. Much to their amazement not a thing even looked at Lex. He garnered a sideways glance from the soldiers around the train here and there as they battled with the sky bombing monsters waged on.

"Alright people, One at a time on me." Sergeant Coleman didn't even say the order at full volume as they were terrified to even spook anything into looking their way at this point. They watched as Lex made it to the train and was lifted onto the main car.

On the bluff above the trail of straggling men and women Junior was struggling to gain consciousness. There was smoke and settled debris from the limestone that had been blown away. Junior started coughing and his heaving was shaking the brush he landed in. He was trying to get up on his hands and knees. The cliff was to his back. He heard some wrestling and commotion to his right some ways off.

"YOU LITTLE SHIT! I'LL KILL YOU!" Issac was screaming as loud as he could. And sounded like a bear tearing through the brush. Both had survived the blast. Both had concussions, but they were both alive and better off than those below. He looked deranged. His eyes were wide with rage. His jacket and under shirts had burnt holes all over the right side with bloodied wounds riddled throughout. His face and exposed skin was mostly black with ash or tan with limestone dust or caked in blood and both. His lower jaw was exposed and you could see the blood and teeth in a grisly sight of what explosives can do. He was unaware of his wounds.

"You can hide, but I'll find you sooner or later." he was a mad man on a mission. Junior had to hide or escape. Playing dead certainly wasn't going to work. Where was Mr Frank with weapons? "I am gonna mess you up so bad, tinkerbell. I am going to slowly beat you to death then throw you off this cliff." Issac went quiet for a little bit as he wrestled through the shrubs. "Here Pussy Pussy Pussy." Issac started taunting Junior as he searched the area.

"So that dude sucks, my guy" Mr Frank joked around as he poked his head through a brush magically like a void in space time to place it right in front of juniors. They were low in the brushes. They were getting further and further away from Issac as his search took him in the opposite direction of them. His featureless face looked at Juniors sideways. "Ahh My Dude?"

"SHHHHH." came the harsh response from the beaten and tired junior. "He'll come back and kill me." Junior had tears in his eyes from the pain.

"My man. It's ok to cry, let it out. Want some Percocet and speed pills? Kill this douche cake and then we can slaughter a witch my guy?" The Shadow person presented a hand and from two fingers came a pill bottle of each.

"Oh god Mr Fank, thank you so much." Do you have a gun?" Junior was leaning a little too far over and fell into the brittle stack of dead brush.

"Oh shit my guy. Here you go. Might want to think fast though." Mr Frank dropped a SIG M18 handgun on the ground next to Junior and phased back through the bush.

"Got you now! you little bitch!" The sound of that sentence and the charging of Issac through the shrubs and undergrowth was enough to scare Junior into vomiting. He started shaking and convulsing all over the ground, heaving and vomiting all over his hands as he reached for the SIG. He inadvertently covered the SIG in mud and vomited while acquiring it. As he gripped it in his hand he saw the hulking Isaac over him and he froze as if he was dead. "Don't tell me this little shit is too far gone to know what I am about to do to him."

He grabbed Junior by the collars and lifted him and put him over his shoulder. He turned and started for the bluff. Junior gripped the pistol and released the safety. He waited as Issac cursed and struggled his way towards the bluffs edge. Junior cocked the gun. Issac heard the sound too late.

"What the?" He said this knowing exactly what it was. It was the sound of his own SIG's chamber being loaded and shot into his back. Though he never heard the shots fire.

Junior pulled the trigger. A mistake, if he had heeded his training, stayed calm and squeezed it. It might not have been so sloppy. He fired two shots into the back of Issac with no problems. The gun went off fine, the 1st shot straight into his back at what Junior thought was a good angle and the second one was wild and off to the side. But it did make contact with Issac just not near any vitals.

Issac dropped saying something pointless about it. He hit the ground like a sack of bricks. Slamming Junior's face and elbows into the ground hard. Sending lighting throughout Junior's skull to compliment the pounding headache he had from the explosions and ass beatings. He rolled around in the ground moaning and crying. Mr Frank moseyed up in a strut past Issac's body giving it a swift kick in the side. He was doing a disembodied whistle.

"Wow, my man you screwed this dude up! I am so proud of you! MY GUY! YEEHAW!" Mr Frank was in a great mood. "Oh my dude, it's ok you can cry. I like it when you do that shit. You want to eat some pills and go try to kill this witch?" Mr Frank crouched down on his hind legs and sat there on them bouncing up and down subtly. He waved a void black hand in front of the face of the crying Junior and produced two bottles of pills. "Pain and speed my dude." Junior stopped in his mid roll and sniffled.

"Really Mr Frank? Junior wiped Snot from his face. "You're the best."

"Seriously, my guy. We have got to go south. Mr Bill sent those guys because we didn't go kill the witch. Now before you get mad. They were supposed to get us back on course , my dude. Not to try to kill us." Mr Frank was carrying on walking in a circle waving one hand in curls as he talked. Junior was shuffling around in the pill bottles trying to get his drug fix.

"Mr Frank a hand please? And some water" Junior was still on the ground in the mud looking up at Mr Frank when he asked mud and tears streaking down his face.

"You look pathetic. Of course my guy. Only thing is water and organics don't come through the voids of my suit. So we need to find water on the way." A fresh set of tears started to well up in the eyes of Junior and he sobbed at the notice of no way to take his pain killers and amphetamines. "My guy! You are such a little bitch with the tears I love it." Mr Frank turned heel in a flashy spin and sat down to watch Junior cry. He reached out to open the child proof containers Junior was struggling with. He opened them with ease. "There is a puddle of water right there my guy." Mr Frank handed the bottles back. Junior scooped up a handful of the fowl muddy water not noticing it was half Isaac's blood. He eagerly swallowed a handful of mixed pills.

Below the bluff and the last of the Army's men loaded back on to the train. As the heavily armored war machine fired up and rolled off back south for the Arsenal the harpies curled en masse in the air above the beach next to the bluff and partly collapsed cliffs. The train ride was silent. Except for the second to last car.

"What the actual hell Baal! You're a freaking Major!" Lex was trying to keep his emotions in check. "Full life? What the hell does that mean? He is missing two limbs, Baal." The exhausted doctor sat down from the whirlwind of explosive questioning that had just ended. The train was rumbling along back to base. Baal and Lex had been alone since the Doctor got on the train. Mostly it was Lex yelling questions and random things. With Baal waiting for him to stop so he could talk. It seemed the time had come.

"My Dear Doctor, It is unfortunate that Captain Gabriel was so badly injured. But he will live a full life. We will send him to high command and their medical center immediately for treatment. With prosthetic technology where it is for them he will come back able to live a full life. Ok? Do you understand what I am telling you about your brother doctor?" Baal sat there in his jump seat bobbing with the train movement. He was dressed as a major and very regal to all he looked like an old man. To Lex he looked much older and more demonic. A version with a crown instead of a military cap. He for certain looked dead serious.

"Baal what High Command? Who has any tech like what you speak of?" Lex did not sound at all skeptical, more curious.

"The Military and a Pseudo America Government is running the Central Band Lex. They have a High Command and you have a United States of America President under the Colorado Desert." Baal paused to see what kind of questions would come from that statement.

"Under the airport no doubt." It was one flat statement from the Doctor and Baal continued on neither confirming nor denying the statement.

"The Knight brothers are very important to the plans of the United States of America. Dr. Lexington Knight. You are extremely important to me. Do you understand why I am telling you this?" Baal was still in his small jump seat, arms crossed body bobbing with the movement. Eyes locked on Lex.

"You want me to understand a few things from it. Some I get and I'm sure some I'm not seeing yet" Lex was thinking, his head was aimed down between his mud and blood covered brown pants. He was playing with a button on his long black coat. "One. That I have power over the people who seek to control me and my brother.

Two. To get what I want now I will need to get what you want. Or slash and what they want. Three. There are a lot of wildcards in this situation so we need to play things close to the chest." Lex looked up from staring at his boots and over at Baal to his left. Baal Smiled evilly at him.

"Lex, I do believe you and I are going to do just fine. Tell me what did you see there? Harpies don't actually exist, Lex they are an illusions made by powerful magick users as a defensive or offensive move." Baal leaned a little in as the new conductor was laying on the train horn the closer they got to the villages and the Arsenal.

"We got there, it was madness we were quickly forced towards Orla's Run...and.." Baal cut him off quickly..

"I'm sorry Orla's Run?" Baal's interest seemed to have peaked at this reference to the cave system below in the bluff of the valley.

"Yes, the limestone cave system in the valley walls there is called Orla's Run. Some explorers named the Saum brothers made the discovery way before The Event. There was some huge seismic event that caused a huge cave collapse. They found celtic artifacts that went to a local museum and everything. It was a huge thing locally. From the wealth they went on to look for Hy-basil. Look Baal, when we got to the beach and the rubble of the opened cave system I made a circle to protect us..." Lex was starting to trail off as he was trying to recall details.

"You're doing great, Doctor. The skill you showed with that circle was quite impressive and I'm not just saying that. Those stones were melted into puddles…" Baal trailed off little this time realizing he might have been in an insensitive manner since it was only the Doctor's brother the circle managed to miss, a mistake of his brothers not of the Doctors.

"Baal, It wasn't the harpies that were the only problem, we got attacked from the cave by, I don't know…We also saw dark shadows of people fighting on the bluff, they even threw explosives at one point.." Baal cut in, Lex hadn't even gotten to what the real problem was.

"Shadow people you say? Fighting with people? I got reports of MOP in the area and there was an explosion high on the Bluff that blocked us from seeing what was up there. Lex the Shadow People of stories are as real as I am and very evil." Baal stopped there to let the Doctor finish.

"Wait, What the What? Shadow People? Look Baal. The Ridge, The Harpies they didn't matter at the end it was what came from the cave that obliterated everything on the beach not in the circle. One blast and everything was dusted." Lex got very distant as he stared off into the metal rivets of the floor. "It started as light coming from the cave then it appeared it was just a big ball of smokeless fire. It was a plasma ball. But alive almost. It was as if it was bothered by the war so it blasted us to hell." Lex just kept staring at the rivets.

"My dear Doctor Lexington, I know what is going on. We will need to move faster and with more force than expected. For unseen enemies have been ahead of us." Baal's crown was wobbling as the train trip was getting turbulent. "I will tend to your brother and mobilize the army and turn them back to the site." Lex groaned in pain at the thought of what was coming as he put his head in both his hands on his knees. "You will need to go meet with Lady Rivers, I'm sure she is aware of who and what Orla is. Meet with her and get her up to speed, we need to get Orla out of there and on our side, but at least out of there. I can meet with you guys through the card to hear your plan to extract Orla." The expression on Baal's face was fierce. Lex sat back straight and breathed in deeply. He remembered he promised himself to see this through. But his gut feeling was telling him a lot of bad things at that very moment.

"Baal just fix my brother I'll get Orla out of there. I'll call you with the how on The Emperor Card. You send a Toad? with the same. Deal?" Lex sat back and worked on his breathing, his arms crossed. He concentrated on nothing but the sensation of breathing.

Chapter Fourteen: Judgment

Byran, Mr Alan and Mr Bill had all been walking for some time before they saw the signs of the Pridesmen camp. Smoke, fire, and noise all came rushing at them as they came over the knoll and into line of sight of the encampment. Mr Alan looked at Mr Bill, their featureless faces gave nothing away to anyone watching them, not that anyone was. Bryan was a few feet behind them walking nervously and muttering to himself about Jesus. He wasn't even watching where he was walking.

"Mr Bill what do you think?" Mr Alan finally asked his boss and friend. The light of day wasn't much with the constant darkness of the black clouds. But you could see the shadow people and most of the landscape well enough for a few hundred yards.

"Well Mr Alan I hope your boy here can get us in. We need to get moving. Mr Frank is having trouble with Junior. Looks like things are up to us for now." Mr Frank looked like he was pretending to smoke again.

"Wha...what are you two talking about? Camp? They will probably shoot us all dead" Byran was shaking and starting to cry again.

"Sir please cry. Do you think they will shoot you dead?" Mr Alan's voice perked up when he saw the tears coming on.

"They can't kill us. One way or another the general will end up talking to us." Mr Bill kept acting like he was smoking a cigarette. He was even flicking ashes.

"What are you doing? Are you pretending to smoke?" Bryan asked in his half sobs.

"What? You little shit. I'm not pretending to be doing anything other than to keep you alive. Where I am. I am smoking." Mr Bill flicked his non-existent cigarette. The place where his eyes should have been, glowed red. Mr Alan stepped between the two figures.

"Mr Bill, Ms Bernadette in HR will kill you if she finds out you're smoking in your suit room again. Bryan, how do you plan to get us in there to speak with the general without getting you shot, sir." Mr Alan was cool and level headed.

"Me? what about you guys, they're gonna shoot because of you not me." Byran started to wail tears and fell to his knees. Mr Bill acted like he was lighting up another cigarette and leaned against a stump.

"Sir, you know I love a good crying session, But let's Mr Bill, myself and you face this situation down together. It will be fine sir." He extended his void black arm out to help the young Byran up. Mr Alan proceeded to wipe the dirt and mud off of Byran as best he could. By best, it was a half ass job to show Byran he cared when really he did not. They continued walking the short distance to the entrance of the camp.

"We don't have time to waste. I need this army up there to make that Djinn go nuclear and level this entire area. Before the witch takes the thing to their side or worse the dam creature finds out that there are more of her kind awake in Massachusetts!" Mr Bill was losing patients. Mr Alan turned to Byran to get him moving.

Before long they found themselves several hundred yards from the only real entrance to this encampment being yelled at by two very tired and drugged out guards.

"Hands up! All of you!" yelled one of the terribly dressed men. He was terribly dressed if you were trying to fight in a military campaign. Most of the men in this camp were noted Mr Bill. "Sound the alarm Abbott!" A loud dinner bell started ringing from behind the two men. Mr Bill was shaking his head at Mr Alan. Byran was pissing himself and crying.

"Byran stop being a bitch. Or I'll take over" Mr Bill's voice was harsh.

"Sir, I need you to pull it together for me and talk to these men." Mr Alan was trying to unfreeze the young man before Mr Bill did something out of anger.

The Gun fire was unrelenting for several minutes. Men were building up at the scantily fortified entrance to the less than notable encampment. No one questioned why they were firing or who they were firing at. Men just showed up and started firing. Byran was torn apart in a hailstorm of bullets in the first volley of the first minute. He made barely a sound as the gunfire was so fast and so complete on him he never heard it coming.

"They'll wear themselves out eventually, why don't you wave your arms with a white flag and we can wait for the general?" Mr Bill was standing there bullets went in his body like into water, leaving ripple waves to glide around as the constant bombardment hit him. The bullets exited out the back with the same effect. Mr Alan experienced no difference in the attack from the Men of Pride assault on them.

"Mr Bill, When they do stop I assume you'll take over Sir?" Mr Alan asked because typically Mr Bill let his men lead unless things were pressed and demanded his more direct involvement. Mr Alan noted that Mr Bill was growing extremely impatient.

"Mr Alan we will both need to work our skills on them if we are to get this done fast and efficiently. Time is against us now" Mr Bill looked at Mr Alan. They nodded and waited for the bullets too slow to a stop and the general to show himself. A horn blew, Mr Bill laughed pretty hard at the sound of it. "You can't be serious, This guy just announced himself with an air horn like he was some kind of king." Mr Alan was enjoying the mirth too. They would enjoy helping these men find gruesome deaths.

In the middle of the encampment the General heard the alarm bell and the gunfire. The general was gathering himself and he heard the gunfire building rapidly.

"Jesus Christ man are we under attack really? What are the men firing at?" The general was trying to put pants on while coughing up a storm. The woman in the bed beside him was crying and hiding in the corners of the makeshift bunk. His nearest officer wouldn't face him. Instead he was just outside of his tented room standing at attention answering what he could to the general. When a runner from the gate came in with news.

"Sir? Sir? Where is the General?" The frantic soldier was sweating and shaking. The Officer responded with a nod to the private room he was somewhat guarding. The man got sheepish. They exchanged knowing and disgusted looks. The General yelled from the not so private room.

"Speak up kid. Tell me what's going on?" The general sounded like he was a stand up guy in voice. But from where the two men were standing it looked much different.

"Sir, three men, Showed up, two of them are impossibly dark. Like Shadow Men sir. They would not comply with orders so eventually the men opened fire. The one normal man dropped but the other Shadow people...they ..." The pridesman was shaking, the Officer standing guard put an arm on his shoulder and nodded at him to continue, but the General cut in.

"Shadow men," you say? Pitch black as the night?" You could hear the girl crying. The General started coughing again. "Carry on, Soldier."

"So these shadow men, they are just standing there taking bullets, more and more men show up and start firing and they absorb the shots sir…." His voice got real shaky, the Officer holding his shoulder shakes a little to offer him some resolve. "The bullets go right through them sir. They seem to be waiting for a chance to talk to someone. They don't seem to be armed." The man started to breathe for the first time.

"Well, Officer Roberts. Sound the horn and lead the way." The General came out of the sheet walled room half dressed like he was a mighty lion. What emerged was an old frail man with a dying body. The men did not look impressed at all. The general in his arrogance would never catch on to the fact that he had not impressed anyone in 20 years.

Officer Roberts knew the horn should slow things down as far as excitement levels went. Men continued firing and vying for placement to fire at the Shadow people. Officer Roberts found it hard but not impossible to push his way through the crowd. Once they actually saw who was pushing and who was with him, people parted like the red sea.

"Move it. Move it" Came Officers Roberts call. Followed by.

"That's my boy, fine work, kid" The general was behind still buttoning his camo coat. He was talking to everyone and no one as he was only paying attention to getting dressed. The gunfire had stopped as they arrived at the fortified entrance. Everyone parted and the General came into view of the Shadow People off down the path. He took a hard-nosed look at them. He couldn't read them. So he did the next best thing. He tapped Officer Roberts on the shoulder and whispered in his ear.

"Parlay?" Yelled Roberts as loud as he could "Do you wish to parlay with the General?" He added to make it seem like they had the winning hand in this situation. It did not matter how you phrased it to the shadow people, they knew the score. Mr Bill tapped Mr Alan on shoulder and whispered something into his ear.

"Please. Sir." Mr Alan said in a nice loud tone. "We mean no harm. We have come to help General Daniels." The Shadow people looked at each other and started to slowly walk towards the encampment. The General had been frantically signally and yelling orders to all the men gathered around. Guns that were trained on them had gone down but hands had not gone off triggers. Something the Shadow people cared little for. They redirected the bullets that entered their body at will. It was out of choice that the two shadow people didn't use all of the thousands of rounds fired upon them back at the rag tag group of seccessionst. The wild eye insanity of these men was painted clearly on their faces. The shadow people were loving it.

The General was standing there in front with Officer Roberts who was clearly in denial of what he was seeing. Most of the men were.

"Hello there." The general was eyeing Mr Bill up and down. "Let's talk in my quarters shall we?" He signaled down through the shanty camp to the middle where a grouping of tents were hung together to make the appearance of a grand leaders tent. It Looked like a childs fort in the middle of a wet field. He continued to check out the two incredibly cosmic black shadow men. The General was too self absorbed to notice how the men were reacting to the arrival of the supernatural beings.

"What the…" Came the not too soft response from a man to the generals' right. Quick was the fury and might of Officer Roberts. As he grabbed the man by the collar and said.

"Watch yourself.…" His sentence ended with a bang and several plus more. Literally, the man was holding a gun and it went off. It was a fully automatic AA-12 shotgun with a drum. Officer Roberts was dissolved to legs of standing meat. The legs thudded abruptly to the ground with a thick wet sound. The man holding the shotgun looked around just as shocked as everyone else. Mr Alan held his hands up.

"NOW I LIKE TO PARTY BUT DAMN BOI!" Screamed Mr Alan in a Disembodied voice all the camp could hear, the blood settling on them. Mr Bill was pretending to smoke again. Giving Mr Alan a knowing glance of theirs. The Shadow people looked at the ghost white General Daniels in that very moment the blood was finished showering them. The crowd of men erupted in roars and yells. Men were jumping and shooting guns in the air. They had no idea what they were celebrating.

"Ok Ok, We've had enough fun" General Daniels looked at his guest seriously for the first time. Mr Bill and Mr Alan faced him at this time. Both featureless and imposing. Everyone in camp was enthralled with the revellaly of whatever just happened. Firing guns clueless to the actual danger of the situation. The General started to call out. Then reach out. But only the shadow people were paying attention to him. His most trusted officer was a pile of meat feet away. He was coughing and wheezing. Then clawing and falling to the ground.

Mr Bill and Mr Alan knelt over him in the mud of his own camp. His entire group of men celebrated nothing around him as two shadow people crouched above him. He was going to die right there in the mud of the black cough and no one would ever know. He would never make his mark. He would die a failure.

"Hey you want to die in the mud?" Mr Bill was still looking like he was smoking a cigarette hunched on his hind legs. If he had features General Daniels would see he was enjoying watching him die. "A favor? Not to die in the mud?" He was facing Daniels but when he finished his question he turned upwards towards Mr Alans. Who was on his hind legs across from Mr Bill. Facing him.

"Gee Sir? A whole favor?" Mr Alan never even looked down at General Daniels who coughing fit has him almost at the ground fully now. He just kept his head at Mr Bill. "Sir he has The Cough. It's more than a favor. His men are wild Sir. We are talking about healing him, supplying him. Can he even take us all the way to beating the traitors and Then Silas Mason?" Mr Alan let the name Silas Mason and his traitors hang out there.

"I'll spit on Silas Mason's grave. He took my Army." Came a wheezy response from the General. Gunfire was still exploding around them everywhere. The excitement of the men had not nearly subsided. "I don't wish to die in the mud." He started a violent fit of coughing filled with blood. "These men, I'll trade, these men, more men, the blood of my enemies….. What do you goddamn devils want? I'll give it to you.. if I can have my pleasures and kill my foes. I'll trade you anything." General Daneils was breathing heavily as he half lay awkwardly in the mud slipping ever so closer to the ground with every moment. Clutching his heaving chest. Mr Bill extended a hand out to the general.

"A favor not to die in the mud." Mr Bill void black hand was cold to the touch of General Henry Daneils neck and upper chest. His body froze temporarily to the forgien sensation of the supernatural beings touch. He felt the weakness and poison of the fungal infection in his body being sucked right out of his body and into the hand of Mr Bill. His eyes were wide with amazement at what was happening. For all around him men celebrated nothing. While a micale of their Generals life being saved over a deal made with the Shadow People.

"Wow Sir, Mr Bill here just cured you of the Cough. I believe to humans that is a death sentence." Mr Alan extended his hands to General Daniels and started to help him up. It was within seconds that the general knew he didn't require the help. He shot up on his feet, flexed his arms and limbs. He stretched and he looked around at the hooting and hollering men. Gun fire went off all around him. He felt like he was 20 years old again. "Sir, Shall we discuss plans somewhere more private with the 3 of us?" Inquired a Mr Alan while gesturing to the shanty shacks in the middle of the camp. The General looked at the mess that was Officier Roberts.

"Yes we have much to discuss, this way friends." General Daniels walked ahead of the shadow people; the crowd of men broke ranks as they walked through. Mr Bill flicked his nonexistent cigarette. Mr Bill started talking right away as it was apparent no one was paying them any real attention, not that he cared either. Mr Bill intended to get as many of both sides killed as humanly possible.

"David Daniels Jr tried to kill your scout team. We were able to save three of them. We sent two of the survivors to retrieve Junior, we had one take us here. To talk with you." Mr Bill was looking around the camp shaking his head as he talked, occasionally glancing at Mr Alan. The General cut him off.

"So Junior was a coward and the 3rd guy with you was one of ours? My men, much like they did Officer Roberts there, blew him to pieces rather than be bothered to ask questions?" The General didn't even look at Mr Bill when cutting off and addressing him. Mr Bill had lost his patience for humans when had to bring Isaac back from near death. Now he was carrying this guy's Black Cough around being cut off like he was this guy's soldier. Mr Bill reached forward and touched his hand on General Daneils neck.

"Listen here, you ever cut me off, piss me off, look at me wrong, don't do what I say….." Mr Bill paused as he waited for the Black Cough to fully set back into the man's system. When the General started to cough again he continued. "…..ask me if my cigarette is real, or basically anything I don't care for. Then you will die in the mud within a matter of minutes. Are we clear?" Mr Bill sucked all the Fungal infection back out and the General fell to the ground coughing. Mr Alan helped him up again.

"Yes of course. You have to understand though. The men, we may want to keep appearance up if you want them to follow us to their death." The General was rubbing his neck as Mr Alan helped him to his feet. Mr Alan was brushing the excess mud off of the General.

"Sirs, It's in all our best interest if we start to act like this is the mutual alliance of two armies joining forces. If everyone else sees it like that then we will reap the maximum benefits. Be it the men or our enemies." Mr Alan's logic had both Mr Bill and the General looking at this in a new light. Mr Bill extended a hand to the General.

"I'm Sorry I threatened you General, it's just that your son Junior pisses me off so much. Mr Alan is right, no hard feelings?" Mr Bill and the General shook hands.

"It's ok Mr Bill, I think we can work this out. And Junior isn't my son." The general Turned and stood on a large crate with a bull horn. "Listen up men! Break camp to move to the Central Band for our take over of the tracks! We leave at dusk." The General was offered a hand from Mr Alan but jumped down. "Thank you Mr Alan but holy shit if I don't feel great. I am guessing you need me to tell men what to do, not really to plan? The General didn't look defeated but he did look disappointed.

"O to contrary my dear General, I'm going to tell who is coming and with what, I am going to tell you what we need and what we can provide. What I need you to do is make the plan and lead the battle so we all get what we want in the victory. How does that sound?" Mr Bill was pretending to light a cigarette. General Henry looked at Mr Alan who started shaking his head 'no' at the General.

Chapter Fifthteen:The Magician

Lex was walking along with his companion Ajax as they made their way from the home. Neither was a vision of happiness. They were covered in mud and blood. Beaten and weary. Slow moving and alone. They were dropped off by the train near old downtown before it made its way underground and across the river. They were strolling by The Source book store when they heard a familiar voice.

"Lex! Lex! Are you ok?" Dom was yelling from a window that was open above The Source bookstore. "You look like hell! Hold on." Lex collapsed right there on the sidewalk into a perfect lotus seated position. The move looked intentional. It was anything but. Just pure luck his body was used to going to the ground into that particular seated position. That a free fall kind of just formed that way. Ajax was licking his face before he fully leaned against the wall of the building.

"Ok, I'll wait here….good boy Ajax." Lex wasn't speaking loud. He was petting Ajax and responding to Dom who had already disappeared from the window. Lex was tired mentally and physically. Dom came busting out the front door to the Doctor's left. Ajax turned heel and ran at Dom only to jump and kiss him on the face and hug him.

"Good Boy Ajax, Good Boy" Dom was petting and hugging the massive wolf on his back. "I'll never figure out how you got a wolf to be your pet dog Lex." The older man turned his attention from Ajax back to his friend who was bleeding on the sidewalk. "It didn't go well did it?" a Grim look came over Dom's face. "How about a ride home for you two? My boy is watching the shop. You look like you could use a bath and a few hours in your meditation room. Come on, I'll even take care of washing up ole Ajax for you while you get cleaned up." He helped Lex up and looked him over. "Here take my keys and fire the truck up, It's over there. I'll get my medical kit. You are going to need stitches." Dom patted Lex on the shoulder and walked back into The Source bookstore.

Lex put Ajax in the back of the pick up and got in there as well. He didn't want to get the front cab all messy with blood, shit and mud. It took Dom about 10 mins or so before they were on the way to Lex's house. The trip was quiet and short for a drive but it could have taken a few hours for Lex to walk in his condition. Dom was flabbergasted by the story Lex recounted to him in amazing detail. From the second he last saw Dom to the moment Dom drove him home. Dom seemed able to focus on the work of stitching up the doctor just fine considering all he was hearing.

"We saw some of the explosions even here, Lex, and the reports of harpies have been happening since the Corps of Engineers blew the bluff wide open weeks ago. As surprising as this all seems, Doctor Lex. It really isn't. My father used to always warn of that bluff and what the Saum boys had discovered there. Said there was a portal to the realm of Faeries and all sorts of Magical beasts below the bluff in the caves." Dom finished the last of the stitches on Lex's forehead with a snip of shears. "Well you go take a bath, I'll clean this familiar of yours up. When you are done. Gather what you need. We can load up the truck and I'll take as far as you need to go to see this through. At the very least drop you off at River Manor so I can visit an old friend before, then it sounds like you have a battle to get back too." Dom wiped his hands with a towel and stood up looking his work over.   Lex looked at him and smiled.

"Thank you Dom. You've always been a good friend to the Knight Family." Lex slowly got up from the kitchen table and proceeded to the bathroom on the second floor. Dom and Ajax moved to the exterior to clear the wolf of all the blood and mud he had acquired. Lex wondered how his brother was doing.

Gabriel was in complete darkness; he couldn't move his arms or legs. He was strapped to a table. He knew this because he could feel that he was. There was no light anywhere in the room. He heard the faint sound of electricity running. He could see the showering sparks. Panic started to set in.

"Heeeeelp! Is anyone there! I'm stuck! Help!" He was yelling as loud as he could. He heard his voice carry around the room in a long echo. He was in a large open area. He heard the electricity sound again. "Oh shit, Not here." He started squirming and moving, his motions got more and more violent. As it fully dawned on him he was in the cursed nightmare with the abomination only this time he couldn't move. The eclectic sound came to full life and the room lit up somewhat.

Gabe looked around and noticed when looking down his body at the far end of the room there was the mass of limbs. It had seen him. It was sliding its way by dragging its grotesque body across the concrete floor towards him. Moaning in excitement at the meal it had found. Gabe started to panic. He looked for his arms to grab at the straps. He then came to realize he did not have an arm. He screamed and looked for his other arm. He did not have either limb. He started trying to flail around and in doing so noticed both his legs were gone as well. He was a toraso strapped to a table in a large concrete room about to be fed to a mass of nothing but limbs and mouths. His screams were endless as were the tears streaming down his face. The electricity roared again and complete darkness enveloped him again.

Lady River was floating above the ground near the caulon in the middle most circle of the backyard at River Manor. She was cooking a feast in a large black cauldron. She also had three smaller ones going with spells brewing for the coming battle. Next to her was a partition blocking the view of the third pit, the training pit. Which was now set for a ritual to invoke the Seal of Solomon. A powerful spell requiring the blood of a black cock that has never lain with a hen. As well as many other things.

Pairlut and Szuil were in the first circle close to the house playing and feeding a black rooster by the name of Reginald who seemed to be having a particularly famous time with Imps and familiars all gathered around him. There was food and music being played by a four piece band of Imps. Witch lights of various colors and effects went off in the yard. The group was having a celebration of life for Reginald. For he had agreed to give his life for the ritual.

Lady River was preparing to make a Seal of Solomon on a belt for the use of Lex. It was the only plan she had.

The last thing she expected to hear was some old beat up pickup truck pulling into her drive. The music stopped. All heads turned their attention in the direction of the driveway side of the house. They all heard the rumbling engine stop. They looked at Lady Rivers as a worried group ready to run and hide.

"Calm down my children, it is just Lex, He brought an old friend. Do not hide. Continue with the festivities." She uncrossed her legs and lowered them to the ground. She dusted off her hands. Ajax came bolting around from the car park. Tongue hanging the side of his mouth as he ran. Several familiars, all of them felines, broke off running after him in the epic game of tag that seems to never end between them.

"Lady Rivers!" Lex was yelling as he came around the corner to see the massive party that was going on. "What the what?" Lex's eyes went wide. "I have bad news. We got our asses kicked." He continued looking around till his eyes just stayed with the group of Imps playing instruments for the Rooster.

"Dom, My Dear old Friend how are you?" Lady Rivers' walked to meet them halfway and embrace Dom. Who was also in complete awe of all that was on display in Lady Rivers' backyard.

"Lady Rivers, your house. River Manor is amazing...and the..inhabitants are as beautiful as Lex said." Dom was simply amazed by it all. "I knew there was magic. But this is Magick" He continued to look around.

"Dom, I wish I had more time to catch up. Lex I have to talk to you. We need you to go back as soon as I can finish this ritual with you. I need you to stop the Shadow people. I believe they want to use Orla as a weapon of mass destruction against us all" Lady Rivers was deadly serious and pleaded with Lex almost.

"Lady Rivers, How do you know about Orla? Dom Thank you for the lift. I think it's best if we say goodbye." He turned to talk to Lady Rivers.

"Nonsense Lex, Dom go sit with the imps and Reginald, make yourself at home, Introduce yourself and be merry. Once I am done with Lex he will be busy for hours and you and I can catch up." She grabbed Dom by the hand and led him towards the group of partying Imps around Reginald. She turned to Lex. "I helped hide Orla in those caves, Now I'll help her find somewhere else to go. Our bigger concern is the Shadow People and who might be working with the MOP." This drew a long sign from Lex.

"Shadow People? I fought Harpies. And I saw a huge ball of Plasma. Smokeless fireball. I did see people who were a little dark from a distance on the bluff and Baal mentioned something. But really? I'd be glad to sit down and listen maybe while I eat? Also I can call Baal too. He is going to bring the Army. He knows what

Orla is as well. He mentioned there is a MOP in the area." Lex seemed slightly confused and a little overwhelmed.

"When this universe of light was created the previous one of darkness was effectively pushed 'out'. The beings that lived there are what we call or know throughout the centuries as Shadow People. They essentially want their universe back sans light and humans. This is how I have come to understand them. They are supernatural beings from a previous universe. Their appearance as shadows is due to the 'suits' they wear to be able to interact in this universe. I have in my life worked with them and against them several times. What we need to understand most of all is this Doctor. MOP, Shadow people, FAE, Sidhe or Demons. Whatever. It doesn't matter, the world is vulnerable right now Lex and anything and everything with a little bit of power is going to try to take control of it." She was explaining this to him as she led him away from the party and past the partition that set them away from all that now.

Lex looked around and saw the chopping block and sill for draining blood. He continued looking the whole area was set with tables for the manufacturer of something that requires a sacrifice. Followed by rituals with the blood.

"Doctor Lex when was the last tinme you had sex?" Lady River was dead serious when she asked but Lex was laughing.

"Oh you're serious? Years. Why do you ask Lady Rivers?" Lex had a concerned look on his face. To which the old witch started laughing herself.

"Good" she handed him a sheet of paper. "Think you can memorize this by heart and then meditate on it deeply for several hours?" Lex reached for the paper from Lady Rivers' hand.

"Lady Rivers I can but are you seriously thinking this will work?" Lex didn't look up from the spellcraft he was reading. He was already committing it to memory.

"You know what I'm planning then do you Doctor?" Ask Lady Rivers with a wry smile on her face. She was lifting her legs back up into a sitting position in the air to float again so she could return to spell work.

"I have no idea what you're planning Lady Rivers, But I do know what the Seal of Solomon is. I'm asking if you think it will work?" Lex went to the middle of the sit pit and pulled out his cards from his jacket pocket. "Should we include Baal?" He tossed his coat and bag on a chair placed nearby. He pulled his Rod from the coat and started drawing a protection circle in the middle of the sandpit.

"No need to cat call Baal , meooow…..prrrrrrrrrr" Came the strange feline-like voice from a nearby brush. Out waltz a pitch black cat with demon red eyes strolling towards the two. It had a purple and gold crown half-cocked between its ears on its head. The partition blocked the view of this new cat from any of the others there. "I see we are quite under way with a grand ole plan." The cat stopped at the edge of the sand pit near its stone border. It started cleaning itself. It started choking on something like a hairball. Lady Rivers and Lex exchanged looks.

"Lady Rivers, Baal. Baal, Lady Rivers. It could be worse. He could be a putrid toad whose own zits pop into flies that it then eats while he talks to you." Lex said this and as if magically the cat's choking went violent. Baal the cat started heaving and vomited up a three quarters dissolved mouse that instantly started running away the second it hit the ground with a wet thud. "Never mind." added Lex as he turned from Baal the cat to continue his reading.

"Where are you going, meow!" Beal the cat launched at the undead mouse it had created and pounced it. Rolling around on the dormant lawn playing with its sticky gross mess. "Seal of Solomeow. Is a solid plan. Make Lex invincible to weapons, fire and water temporarily. I'll distract the Harpies and MOP with the Army. I like it, Meow." Baal the cat had ripped the undead mouse in two and both halves were running in opposite directions. He couldn't decide which to pounce first.

" Lex gets through while you and the Army do all the work Baal. He gets Orla and he gets out of there." Lady River was floating next to a table a few feet away preparing what appeared to be multiple pouches of herbs. She was spellcasting over them as she tied the bundles. Krip was spellcasting over a bunch of similar pouches as well. Mostly she was ignoring the sight of looking upon the grossness that was Baal.

"Of Course Meow. I need her out of there and with us. I also need MOP gone so I can get the train with Captain Knight and team to High Command in Colorado." Baal started eating the bottom half of the mouse which he had caught.

"How is my Brother doing Baal?" The Doctor was no longer readying his circle for meditation or memorizing the piece of spellcraft Lady River had handed him earlier. Instead all attention is on Baal the cat who was stalking the other half of a mostly digested undead dissected mouse.

"Under sedation and having fitful nightmares. But he is very strong. He will do fine. MEOW!" Baal the cat leaped, clawed and rolled with the undead mouse torso as he caught it mid roll. On his back and tossing the viseracted mouse half in the air with all four legs Baal continued, his purplish crown still somehow on his cat head. "I need the area cleared so I can get his team to deliver him there for his prosthetic surgeries and all required medical attention at this point. The whole lot went through hell at Orla's Run. They are to be debriefed. Trained, then briefed on the new assignment. Right as they get... meow." At the end of the sentence Baal the cat tore into the mouse toroso and started viciously eating it while holding it with his front paws but kicking it simutantulouly with his hind paws. Gore, slime and entrails were flicked out wave after wave.

"Baal. I'm going there at 2am to clear Orla out and get her here to Lady Rivers. Then I am going back to finish clearing anything or one in the way of getting my brother's train off and on its way to colorado. Anything needs to change, find me, you seem good at that. Are we good?" Lex looked at Baal, the cat who wasn't paying attention to him. "Ajax, here boy." Lex barely spoke it and Ajax came wide from behind everyone out past even their best guest of the yards depths of darkness. He was a bolt of fur and light. "Grab Baal, softly and hold him." Lex said in a calm even manner. Baal was still playing with his sick little treat ignoring Lex. Ajax jaws seized him and wiped him gently around and held him like a mom does her baby kitten by the scruff. Ajax carried Baal the cat hissing the whole way over to Lex, his little kitten crown fell off his head.

"Baal, are you listening?" It didn't seem like you were listening to me?" Lex's emotions were in check, he was breathing fine. He was simply done. "Baal, distract the Harpies and MOP, I'll get Orla the message and to safety. Baal, you and the army fight both fronts till I can remove Orla. I'll return to help finish so the train can get to High Command. When I return I will use the cards to get my brother to High Command if I have to, am I clear? We end this incursion on multiple fronts. Now. We were supposed to be on our way to the east coast already. Let that set in. We are losing on multiple fronts right now. Some of these fronts we are not even aware exist. I've deduced this on my own. After tonight we have to come together as a team or we will lose to all these other forces. Do you guys understand we don't even know what Salem holds? And some of us can't see ourselves living through this." Lex looked at a person. Lady Rivers.

"Lex, are you ready to start your spellcasting side of the ritual?" came the solemn response of the High Priestess. Ajax had a wide smile you could see through the fact that he was still holding one Baal the cat by the scruff.

"Yes, my Lady. Ajax do me a favor, take Baal home. But please escort him safely to hell and be back before I awake from meditation if possible, friend. If it's not possible then I trust you to make the best choice that gets you here by my side when I come to. I'll need your help to get to Orla's Run and make it all the way through." It could be said the wolf somehow had a smile on before as he held the humlitaled demon cat but now, well if there was ever a time in history a wolf or dog ever had a shit eating grin then this was that moment. He turned and bolted with Baal the cat in his jaws off the grounds.

"I hate demons." Said Lady River who was deep in her work. "Lex, are you almost ready to spiritually prepare yourself to meditate? Do you understand the Spell? It's like a prayer you need to reciate deeply to the point of chanting it internally to yourself into a trace until midnight?" She gave Lex a grave look.

"I'm ready. May I meet Reginald 1st please?" The question that Lex just asked was never expected. In fact Reginald was going to meet Lex as he was meditating to avoid any guilt the Doctor may have had at killing this living and self conscious being for the ritual. Something humans never were able to grasp, animals being conscious. Reginald was trying to save him from guilt or pain of this sacrifice.

Lady Rivers said nothing as she floated away. Tears filling her eyes. She wasn't sure what she expected. But it wasn't this. She didn't just hear the request of Lex. She heard the pain in his voice over knowing what he was asking, as he knew without anyone telling him that reginald was going to die to give his blood on the off chance Lex might save all theirs. She heard in his voice that Lex was more concerned with Reginald being ok that he was being sacrificed over Lex. Lex wanted to hear from Reginald that he believed in Lex and this ritual. He didn't care if the others did. Lex wants to know what Reginald believed and wanted. That moved emotions in Lady Rivers as a human that had not moved in her in decades.

"Lady Rivers? Lady Rivers?" Lex looked around, shook his head and sat back down to continue committing the spellcraft of Solomon's seal to memory for his meditation. Moments went by and Lex continued to study the spellcraft. Unbeknownst to him a black cock slowly started to do a slow peck-like scope from around the partition from the far side of its wall which was fairly blowing in the night wind.. Pacing the area back and forth. Behind it, bobbing back and forth. Reginald was nervous.

Lex had become aware of his visitor and went about his work until he finished his last rune in the northern corner of his circle. Then placed the cards in a pant pocket and sat in the lotus position in the middle of the circle again which was slowly warming in color. Resting the cold iron casting rod on the ground to his right. Still within the circle and near reach. It was glowing faintly on one end with a purple hue.

Reginald head bobbed his way shyly out around from the partition and made a little criss-cross path towards Lex. Reginald did a little hop over the stone circle and made his way into the circle pit ever closer to Lex. Who softly spoke to Rginald.

"You must be the famous Reginald, I am Dr. Lexington Knight. It is quite an honor to meet you." Lex stared at the black rooster who stared back at him with his head half cocked to the side taking in all that was the Doctor. Reginald made some cooing noises. "You are very brave to take on this task. To give us a chance to save the area and the people. I wanted you to know I have friends and family here and I am very thankful to you. If there is anything I can do you just ask. You forever have my deepest appreciation for all you're about to give for this world." Lex's eyes started to tear up. He started to wipe them away. When he was done Regnaild was sitting in his lap cooing. Lady Rivers was peeking around the partition when she caught a glimpse of Lex hugging and petting Reginald in his lap. The rooster was snuggling into the doctor's chest and making noises of affection. She turned away crying.

Pairlut and Szuil saw their High Priestess crying and ran to her. When they got to her legs and hugged her they realized she was happy. Szuil turned and looked past the partition blowing in the wind and saw Lex and Reginald embracing each other in comfort. Szuil broke away running to them and embraced them in a big hug. Pairlut followed suit. Dom stood up and walked over to Lady River and held her hand. They watched as Ajax and many other familiars pile on around them to join in the embracing Reginald and Lex. Imps from the band and various other areas of the party and manor came to join the big circle of love. It was the largest sitting group hug in the history of River Manor.

When it was over. Lex would meditate till midnight. Lady Rivers with Szuil and Pairlut would finish the ritual for the Seal of Solomon after sacrificing Reginald under the increasing light of the moon. The rest would finish to prepare the various spells and enchantments for the coming battle to be used by Lex and stock up the manor for any unwelcome visitors. For now Dom and Lady Rivers got to enjoy the love the group was sharing.

Chapter Sixteen: Wheel of Fortune

Junior was full of energy and pain free. Just gliding along the cliffs on his way south along the Mississippi river headed towards the QCA and the villages outside the Arsenal. Mr Frank seemed in good spirits as well. Mr Frank had turned Junior to the color of void black again to camouflage their movements as best they can. Mr Frank had the ability to relay information or parts of information if the circumstances were right back and forth between himself and Mr Bill. Having done so it seemed everyone was headed to the proper places to make their original plan work.

Junior and Mr Frank would wait and watch the witch. While they did this Mr Bill would lead the MOP against the Army in battle from above the bluff with the MOP having the high ground and hopefully those dam harpies aiding them more than not. Mr Alan would take a small group with explosives and infiltrate the caves of Orla's Run. Blow up the river side of the caves and draw out the energy being to the war. When Mr Frank gets the signal that Orla is on the move to destroy the Armies of men, Junior and he will then make their move to obliterate the witch queen and her Coven's Manor. The biggest of the goals for the Shadow people is the removal of what they consider the humans Witch Queen Lady Rivers.

"Is she powerful Mr Frank?" asked a spasmodic Junior. His head was twitching almost as fast and eratactily as his hands were. "Like you are? Or is she even more so? Is she human? Was she ever human?" The questions Junior kept asking were the same ones over and over again for the last 45 mins as they hiked through the dead woods and brush.

"Ooooo, look my guy, it's another fairy ring of massive mushrooms." Pointed out Mr Frank whose head was skyward taking in the mass of the enormous fungi. It was glowing yellow faintly in the areas layered in shadows. "Let's not walk through this one, ok?" asked Mr Frank

"Bad luck Mr Frank?" Junior was scanning all around them in the area as if he was high alert for the "bad luck'.

"Well we crossed through the last one and that didn't end well for us. Let's play it safe. We are after all on the witch's home turf now." They both slowed down their movement and proceeded to move with more intention. "We will be in position to watch and wait for our chance to move soon my man." added a low hunched Mr Frank. "So this is what will happen. I can't kill humans, I can help them to kill themselves or others but never do it myself directly. But I can kill any other creature or entity, spirit or being with extreme prejudice in any way I want. I usually choose the most violent way possible." He put a hand up to stop Junior. Then he sat back on his hunches. Junior did the same. Mr Frank pointed to a large estate just on the next hill.

"That is River Manor where the Witch lives with all sorts of supernatural beings and monsters. You need only focus on killing her. I will watch your back and worry, not my guy. I will kill every Imp, familiar, fly, dog or cat that tries to stop us. Deal?" Mr Fank turned a featureless head towards Junior and they shared a blank look with each other. Mr Frank put his hand on Junior's shoulder. "During the confrontation whatever you need or want like a gun or grenade, just yell it at me and I'll toss it out of my void suit to you. I will also randomly drop you supplies and weapons as it is happening that I think you may need or will need. Sound good?"

"I'd ask what to expect but we have no idea do we? Witchcraft, monsters and fighting? Yea sounds good to me" Junior was shaking but seemed resolved to see this through. It was almost impressive to Mr Frank. Who expected that he would die in an explosion with the witch. "You have the explosives right? How about I set a few blast charges up now and make it really hard for them to even get an attack off on us once we start?" Junior had a wicked smile on his face that complimented the colourlessness of his eyes from being so dilated due to the amphetamines coursing through his blood stream. Mr Frank hands went down and out slid everything that Junior needed to start setting up for his assault on River Manor.

Back on the top of Orla's Bluff three men stop over a dying Isaac. All were staring at him confused as to how anyone could beat Isaac up so thoroughly, especially Junior.

"Well shit. Tony, run and get a medic and cot. Also tell the boys to start setting up a medical tent. We might be able to save him." The man scratched his head. "Look at his face. Jesus, Isaac what the hell did Junior do to you? Now where is Ben and Chris?" He looked around The area. "Men search for any of the others, and find signs of where Junior went. Move it!" Men scattered.

Turning around, the loan figure looked back to the coming caravan of Pride Man. They were a little less than hundred and fifty now. But with the high ground and the help of the shadow people and their supplies they had the upper hand from here. The Central Bands Army of Northern Aggressors didn't stand a chance if they tried to fight them on the bluff. Only way to approach the MOP position for the Army was going to be below from the tracks and the river.

Two Shadowy figures, one in a brimmed hat and long coat the other a nondescript shadow each walking on opposite sides of General Daniels approached the edge of the bluff. Men all around and behind them were shouting and receiving orders. Setting up defenses and unpacking crates of munitions and weapons.

"Well my cosmic masters, What do you think? We have a solid plan. Now we just need to get Mr Alan and a group in the caves and get the Army up here with that train of theirs." General Daniels was looking mighty satisfied this was going better then his most wild of dreams.

"Once their men arrive and start shooting the Harpies circling above, spring the attack. Once it starts, Mr Alan will commence his operations and Mr Frank will commence his. I will stay with you and ensure the battle is won here, everyone clear?" Mr Bill flicked a pretend smoke over the edge of the bluff.

"Roger." came the General's response.

"Sir, Ms Bernadette from HR, just came by and she was asking about the mission." Mr Alan was whispering in Mr Bill's ear.

"Mr Alan, not now" The tone of Mr Bill's Voice changed to one of solid annoyance. Something he had been experiencing from multiple fronts for the last few days. The sound of the train's horn leaving the Arsenal could be heard in the distance.

"45 mins people. MOVE IT! MOVE IT!" came calls from multiple lead officers in the ragtag group of Men of Pride now swarming the bluff in preparation to try and overwhelm the army and steal their train. Or so the Pride thought, the Shadow Peoples real plan was to get Orla out in the battle and have her nuke both sides and as much of the surrounding area into molting ash and rock. Plain and simply destroy all magical and human competition in the northern American continent. So they can quietly and safely strip River Manor and everything or one attached to it until they find the items they need to to bring more of their kind back to this world.

By the time Lex woke from his deep transcendental meditation of the spellcraft he memorized the party was cleaned up and put away. Many of those in attendance had gone back to chores or their amulets to rest. Or were simply off doing something out of sight. Ajax was nearby sleeping in a pile of furry familiars in the far corner of the yard. Lex stretched and yawned deeply before standing up. He looked around. All the stuff that was there to be used on Reginald to make the seal was cleared up and gone.   Sadness overcame the Doctor. What a brave rooster. Lady Rivers was asleep in her chair close by holding a belt with a fine parchment woven into it. The parchment had the Seal of Solomon drawn on it in the virgin blood of Reginald the rooster. Dom was in the chair next to her fast asleep snoring. He had a pot bellied imp sleeping on his lap sideway and Krip was sawing z's in the air with magical symbols as he slept on Dom's shoulder. Lex smiled deeply at the scene.

"Lady Rivers, I must leave now." With that Ajax shot up sending furballs meowing excitement flying in all directions. He came running across the yard to sit at attention next to his master. "Good Boy Ajax, Lady Rivers, It's time." He reached to touch her shoulders but she looked at him and spoke.

"Good way to lose an arm." she was smiling widely at the jest. "Wrap this tightly under everything else in your waste. No weapon, fire nor water will harm you as long as you wear it. Till midnight tomorrow. If it rips the spell breaks." She was wrapping it around Lex and staring him in the eye. "How many of your mothers books did you get to read?" there was nothing but cold calculations in her questions.

"Actually quite a bit, and before you ask, I understand some of it quite famously. Other concepts are quite foreign. Why do you ask Lady Rivers?" Concern showing Lex's voice.

"We are going to need every bit of magic and fight knowledge you know to make it through this Lex. I'm glad you can understand quite a bit. I made a bunch of spell pouches. They all have varying effects, I wrote the spell you say to activate it on the pouch. You say it into the pouch then toss it at the target. The spell title says what its effects are. Does that make sense?" She handed him one of the pouches. It read across the top. Love, followed by the arcane spellcraft phrase.

"Love? Like a love spell? So I say the spellcraft tosses it on a guy and he loves me?" Lex looked weirded out by this. Lady Rivers started laughing. Krip farted loudly and the three sleeping occupants next to the witches started shuffling in their chairs. Lex and Lady Rivers giggled.

"Lex if you tossed this at a guy with say a flame thrower then he fell in love with you right? You say please help me! They want to hurt me. He then turns on everyone else with the flames to protect his true love." Lady Rivers gave Lex a 'Huh what do you think now' look. To which Lex started laughing.

"You are absolutely diabolical. Are there any pouches that are more like fire, ice and lightning? Something I might not need to be so creative with?" Lex was looking around at the Manor as he was trying to form a plan of approach for the bluff in his head. He heard the train horn blare as it was leaving the station. "Crap I'm gonna be late to the party"

"Lex here is a bag you'll find about 60 pouches with an assortment of nasty surprises in there. Take the cards and your rod. I don't think you will need much else. When you get to Orla, make a Circle and do Reiki on yourself while in the circle talking to her about who and why you are there, That I have sent you. Explain what has happened from The Event to the battle you'll be fighting at that moment. I know she will come to reason. Be safe" With that they hugged each other deeply.

"Hey now wait a second I want a hug too." came Dom's Sleepy voice. "You missed one hell of a party Lex." he joined the embrace. "I heard you're late. What's you say I give you and the old wolf here a lift as close as I can get yea?" Lady River's and Lex were about to say no when a familiar cat meow came from behind.

"I need you right Meow, Lex, Meow. you're late. So how about that guy giving you a lift and I'll make you guys invisible?" The cat was sitting there chewing a still moving undead mouse. "Obviously you'll be visible as soon as you attack something when you get there but your buddy and you can get in safe and he can get out safe. purrrr" Baal the cat was cleaning himself awaiting the answer. "You guys are missing out this shit tastes delicious." Baal the cat continued licking his neither areas.

"Baal make us invisible. Truck and all. Dom lets roll." They all loaded in the truck. Lex pulled the Baal card and asked his wish. Then they pulled off and flew down the hill to head off to the battle. Hopefully only fashionably late.

"You see that my guy?" Mr Frank asked, pointing at the truck leaving with the last of the actual humans from the manor. "Their greatest fighter just left to go fight your dad at the bridge site. The manor is quiet. Most of the Imps and creatures are back in their amulets and the Witch Queen is alone, my dude." Mr Frank was rubbing his hands together and he got up and started walking up the short hill to the top so he could go over and around and come back down from above the manor when they made their approach to attack it.

"Wait Mr Frank." Junior called out. Mr Frank turned around.

"Last time you waited Mr Bill sent people who tried to kill you. There is no waiting Junior we go do this now or I am leaving my guy. I'm not pissing Mr Bill off again." Mr Frank turned and continued walking.

"Mr Frank I just want drugs so I'm high when I do this please? I'm more likely to cry after I'm all high." pleaded the young Junior with Mr Frank.

"Ok my guy. you know I can't say no to you. Or getting to watch people cry." He waved his hand back and forth in front of Junior's face until a couple bottles popped out. "Enjoy my guy." Junior eagerly grabbed them and started the process of eating his favorite drugs. He followed Mr Frank on his criss-cross path up and over to the next hill to cut down and through the thick brush there so they could surprise attack Lady Rivers and River Manor.

Lady River was laying back in her chair breathing deeply trying to rest next to her Imps who were sleeping in the dormant grass one on each side. Krip her smallest imp was hidden away in his favorite hiding spot. She was so exhausted she didn't hear the man or his fowl shadow fiend companion enter their sanctum right away. She heard the thud of something hitting the ground next to her and then again further behind her. She got up and looked behind her. There was a bundle of something near the corner of the back porch that was fizzing with flame. Another thud next to her hit the ground.

"Szuil! Pairlut! We are under attack!" she screamed. As soon as she did, a brilliant explosion rocked the entire estate of River Manor. From the darkness of the tree line came two figures. Junior and his shadowy companion Mr Frank. Smoke and fire were still blowing wildly through the area.

" Woooooohoooo ! How about that Mr Frank? Boom dead witch." Junior was peacocking around with explosives in his hands while Mr Frank was scanning the area.

"Holy shit, my guy." They were both still taking in the carnage when they heard some coughing. An unnatural wind blew through. It was so fast and harsh it blew out the fires and removed all smoke. Floating in a large charred area with a half blown away collapsing house behind her was Lady Rivers. She was completely scratchless, no dirt, char, or blood. Not even her hair was slightly messed up. Around her was blood and pieces of Imps. The look on her face was that of pure revenge. The circle she was floating above was glowing gold and had many runes around changing in and out of a multitude of colors.

"You killed my Imp friends. Boy." her hands were making motions and her lips moved in spellcraft softy.

"Oh shit, Mr Frank gun please?" Junior turned to Mr Frank who was staring at the terrifying sight of the Witch as she was building power. "Mr Frank?"

"Nothing can save either of you now Junior." The threat from Lady Rivers sent chills through everyone there.

"I was supposed to kill the battle Imps Junior and you the witch Queen? Not the other way around my guy." Came the stammering words of Mr Frank.

"Oh Mr Fank you can still have a go at my battle Imps, They've been waiting to show you their toys. As for you, you killed two of my Imps, they were dedicated musicians who did not deserve that." Junior was trembling, pissed himself and fell to his knees crying. "Can you swim Junior?" Krip came out from inside the blouse pocket of Lady river dagged dress. He was upset and holding a pouch. "I understand you like women and drugs. To see and experience them. We have lots of those here in the Central Band." Lady Rivers was moving closer and closer to Junior. Junior was turning more and more into a blubbering mess of nonsense about how sorry he was.

"Don't let her near you my Guy!" yelled Mr Frank as he made his way to junior to break the spell he was under. He made it about three steps before from behind an Imp jumped on his back and dug a vibrating dagger deep into Mr Franks shoulder. The unnatural sounding wails Mr Frank let out were not of this world. The blade was an enchanted gift from the High Priestess that was made for killing special entities whose weakness was harmonically based. It was a cross between saser technology and a dagger. Szuil held on for dear life as he twisted and slammed the blade further and further into the creature's shoulder.

"Ahhh, you little shit, What the Hell!" Mr Frank screamed and reached to pull off the Imp with his free working arm but right as he did. Pairlut appeared out of nowhere seemingly and took the sister dagger to Szuils and jabbed it all the way through the forearm of Mr Franks free right arm. The daggers' constant harmonic vibrations were causing cracks and leaks to break and flow from the daggers entry point outward. Interdimensional aether leaked from the wounds into this realm. Mr Frank shaked wildly, screaming wails of pain and frustration at how quick things went south.

"Come here my son, let me help you up." Lady rivers extended both arms to help the balling Junior to his feet. He was crying about how sorry he was as he rose upwards with Lady Rivers saying "I know I know." He looked her in the eye and she said "This is the last thing you will ever see." With that Krip threw a pouch in his eyes while the Lady recited the spell. The pouch exploded in his face and the acid ate away his eyes, optical nerves, muscles and facial tissue. He went to the ground screaming and clawing his sockets which were filled with goo and acid. This only aided in melting flesh from his fingers and more from parts of his face.

"I'm not going to kill you, but I am going to give you the option of not having to fight to live. If I ever see you again I'll take your hearing, then your taste, then your smell." With that lady Rivers pulled a twisted red colored wood casting wand out of her cuff and with a flick and a spell cast. She had Junior floating in the air above her screaming and clawing his face. His hands are meatless, tendons and bone now. She did a full body movement that sent her forward towards the river. It also sent Junior flying out of control spinning end over end into the black water of the immensely wide and deep Mississippi river. She turned to see how her Battle Imps were doing.

"Pin him to the ground boys." Lady Rivers' tone was sinister sounding. "Krip more acid please." Krip disappeared into his hiding spot to retrieve his supplies. Pairlut and Szuil kept their daggers firmly in the shadow man. If he seemed to be able to start gaining control or movement they would twist the blades. The wailing would begin. Slowly it was wearing the shadow man down.

"Please stop, I'll do anything, Just stop. It's over. Please" Mr Frank collapsed to the ground with a thud and the Imps still well attached. Daggers were still humming and deep in him. Aether oozing out. The cracks seem to grow longer and longer down his arms and back.

The Imps held position on top of him now holding him down and using the angle and leverage of the daggers to ensure this dominance. Lady Rivers came into view above Mr Frank she was holding some of Krips acid pouches.

"You tell Hatman, That he has declared war. Do you know what Void Sickness is?" Lady Rivers was waving the pouches over Mr Frank.

"Void Sickness? What are you talking about? We have no such thing as illness in my world." Mr Frank was very defiant.

"See there you are wrong. Open his wounds wide." Lady Rivers said this then immediately added something to the two pouches she held. She started spellcraft over them. Mr Frank started wailing as the Imps twisted the daggers for maximum crack width in the suit armor of the shadow man. "Watch your hands my dears." Then she tossed a pouch each on the dagger sights and the acid popped and filled the wounds and cracks and bubbles as it made its way in. Mr Fanks started screaming and writhing so much the imps jumped away with daggers in hand. "Go to your masters and tell them you have broken an eons long treaty" Then they turned away from the screaming monstersority.

The three looked back upon their half destroyed home and yard. Mr Franks screams disappeared as he vanished from the area the second they turned away. The roof collapsed on one of the remaining sides of the home. Lady Rivers patted both her Imps on their backs simultaneously.

"Good job boys, you two really gave that shadow guy the business. Sorry I didn't sense them sooner." The three of them hugged. Szuil sobbed for his lost brothers.

Chapter Seventeen: Justice

The Army train pulled into the site below Orla's Bluff with not so much as howl of the wind. The men filed out of the train once it came to a full stop and the Conductor had given the go ahead. It was then that higher ranking officers started shouting orders and lower ranking men came filing out and into defensive positions around the train. Men slowly started covering maneuvers up the ruined beach and collapsed bluff area.

On the Bluff above Mr Bill walked down the line of hidden men. His hand was out reached and each man he pasted it shot out a fully loaded ready to go RPG he did this down a line of ten men.

Then he turned around, walked back and gave each man a fully loaded RPG to fire after that one was exhausted.

"After the snipers get the Harpies to attack the beach. I want you boys to take those gifts Mr Bill has provided us and blow that train and every close group of men you see down there to pieces." The General was ecstatic. He nodded at Mr Bill who walked off the other way towards another group of men on the bluff. "Anyone here without any particular order. Just fire on the enemy at will once the rockets go off." The General turned and waved his hand at the sniper up on the hill. The Sniper took several fast shots in succession high in the air. He was plucking off Harpies flying high in the sky above the beach.

Then came the screeches. First the distant ones of the now dive bombing harpies. Followed instantly but a row of RPGs fired from the bluff. Rocket propelled grenade after grenade hit the side of the train cars sending it over on its side car by car. Fire, smoke and blood filled the air with men's screams. The Harpies landed hard grabbing still burning men, some of them actively firing guns into the monsters as they were carried off. The second set of ten RPGs in row were hitting the beachfront assault of the army while the Harpies were still picking men up screaming and before anyone even could register what the heck happened.

Mr Bill was strolling past the new group of men he had been dishing RPGs out watching the mass carnage unfold on the beach below. Hoping Mr Alan was ready to blow the caves now.

"I have to get Orla first Dom!" yelled Lex from the rear of the truck. "So, This will work right?" Lex didn't have time to be nervous but he was.

"Sure as shit son. I'm going to pull right to the moss covered wall, I'm telling you it's just growing over the entrance to the door to Orla's Run. The Saum Boys even carved it on the entrance in Runic. You'll see it. Jump out and run straight, never turn unless it's right. You'll come to Orla and the battle in no time." The truck came tearing around a corner. And slid to stop right up against a wall of moss hanging over the wall.

Lex went to get off the back of the pickup and as he went to jump he noticed the group Pridesmen standing there with a shadow person. The Doctors eye went wide, he forgot he was invisible and moved on reaction. He reached in the bag Lady Rivers gave him. He pulled a pouch labeled Intense Fire Burn. He read the spellcraft and tossed it.

"Surprise boys!" The ball of flame burned bright hot and covered the five men fully melting them to ash and goo. The Shadow man stood there looking at the smoldering bodies and then at the truck with Lex on the tailgate and back and forth a few times.

"Surprise indeed, Sir. Bravo. I'm Mr Alan and who may I ask are you?" Mr Alan did a little bow.

"I have this!" Lex pulled out this Cold Rod and started chanting Rieki like Lady River instructed him to do upon arriving at the caves. The Rod started to glow with cosmic light and energies swirled around it. "DAI KU MYO." Mr Alan's head turned ever so slightly.

"Well , My Sir you are the most impressive human I've come across in decades. Where did you get such a device?" Mr Alan recognized it as a saser, the same type of weapon that destroyed his suit once before and almost killed him. A suit he just got back from maintenance. "Well, enjoy the explosion then." and with the comment Mr Alan blinked from existence. Leaving behind the bundles of explosives they had with them only they were lit. Mr Alan hadn't lit them, it was Lexs own doing that led to this.

Lex already had a card in hand, the perfect card. It was the 10 of Cups, the card of Glasya-Labolas, a large hellhound with enormous wings like a griffin. Lex called him forth instantly demanding he carry the truck and its occupants to safety.

"As you wish summoner." Came the cruel voice of the demonic creature, yet it was eager to please Lex. With massive claws it instantly grasped and lifted the truck off and into the air. Dom screams at the top of his lungs for the mercy of god. "God has left you for now, old man." Came demon hounds' response as it lifted them up into the fray of harpies above and near the river.

"Dom I promise you I will get you out alive friend." Lex started to rifle through the cards looking for the only demon he thought could help them now that they were above the river. The Harpies started barraging the winged demon hound with clawed hits of fury. Taking chunks of flesh and howls out of the beast with each hit. It wouldn't be long before he would drop them or the truck just fell apart. As the Harpies were grasped onto it as well tearing at the cab and bed trying for the human men. Lex found the card and put it between his teeth. Then quickly grabbed a pouch. Smoke Eternal. He read the spellcraft and blasted the biggest harpy holding on to Glasya-Labolas.

It was enveloped with impenetrable smoke that stayed pinned to its center point of mass following its movements anyway it went. It fell off in a frantic dive to the waters below wailing. Smoke stayed dead center of it the whole way. Lex turned while ready another pouch. Crystalline Structure. Lex chuckled, read the spellcraft and nailed another Harpy attacking Glasya-Labolas via airstrikes in mid-flight.

The streaks of lighting shot out in all directions from the pouch pieces all foes of the group within a 30 meters circle of them in the air. They miss Glasya-Labolas, Dom, Ajax, and Lex completely. Over a dozen were impaled in the now floating Crystalline Structure. It fell silently to the rushing river below.

"Sire more will be on us I must lower you, I see you have Sallos card in your mouth he can be trusted summoner, Ask him of his 30 legions. He will take you to land and to victory. I will finish the Harpies for good. Ok Master?" The demon looked at Lex. Lex instantly removed the card and spoke the words.

"Glasya-Labolas Thank you, my friend, good battle. you may drop us here" Lex waved him clear. The truck hit with a splash and started to sink.

"Lex what the hell man!" Dom was freaking out more than any man Lex had ever seen freak out.

"Dom, I understand but I need you to be calm so I can keep my promise to get you out of this alive." Lex pulled Dom out of the cab and Ajax let Dom get on his powerful back for support. A large seprepant-like movement in the river bumped the truck twice. It was a giant gator roughly 15 meters brushed by the three of them. Twisting its way around silently in the black river waters. They all jumped. But before they could scream a soothing voice of a man sitting on the gator's back spoke.

"Greeting friends, I'm Sallos, your ride to hell this evening. This is Deinosuchus, my trusted steed, he makes sure no harm befalls any of you " The demon let out a charming laugh that went with his handsome looks and upper class mannerisms. Ajax was already on the great gators back shaking away water from his thick coat of wolves hair. "Summoner, it's a pleasure to meet you. The last card holder was a tyrant. I take it we are going to the fire and bloodshed on the beach Sir?" Sallos was by far the most peaceful and charismatic of all the demons Lex had met so far. He also looked just as fierce as any.

A man clad in ornate spiral pattern armor of emerald greens that held no seams or breaks in it, as if there was no kink in his armor. He sat high in a saddle upon the mighty demonic gator with a lance in several meter length and heft. It was resting in the crux of his shoulder. His long hair was changing from black to orange and back and gave off an aura that changes from gold to silver respectively. He was angelic in many ways. He continued talking as the crocodile silently stalked its way to the shore and the mighty war being waged there.

"My Lord we don't have much time, There are benevolent and malevolent spirits attached to those cards. Some serve god, some themselves, others serve higher powers. I am of a group in the cards that serves benevolent leaders and summoners for good. We fear god. That said, most of us can read the hearts of men. I will serve you with all my legions and wish you to trust me as your field commander when we hit the beach." The beach sight was fast approaching as Lex and Dom watched one of the last group of soldiers go up in a volley of RPG fire. They exchanged looks of fear.

On the Bluff above Mr Bill was smoking his non-existent cigarette. Enjoying the bloodshed. Before he could wonder about the other shadow people Mr Frank appeared screaming while clutching his left shoulder and arm as best he could in a dance of pain and howls.

"Mr Bill! That witch...her Imps had Harmonic daggers. They pierced my suit like Saser technology, Then the little shits held the wound open while the witch dropped acid into the wounds..help me Mr Bill..It's melting through my suit to the other side." He was screaming and writhing in pain. Mr Bill looked over the wounds. He saw the Aether releasing from the cracks as the acid worked its way in.

"It is important Mr Frank, What else Did Lady Rivers say?" Mr Bill had the red glowing orbs in his head again. Mr Frank was trying to stay calm but knew he was in more trouble than any Shadow person had ever been in when he saw those red orbs.

"She told me to tell you that you started a war, then she asked me if I knew what Void Sickness was. She melted Junior's face and sent it flying off into the river. Please Mr. Bill I can't Jump home for medical attention. Something is preventing me. Help me.`` Mr Bill leaned down to get closer to his friend.

"They won't let you come home, You'll spread it faster in our realm. And as long as you are alive here you will slowly spread in your body back in the suit room, till it consumes you. Then you'll die terribly and it will spread across what's left of our pocket dimension. So, they haven't ordered me to kill you yet. I'd run for now. That's the best I can do Mr Fank. Other than kill that Witch queen for what she did. Because sooner or later Mr Alan is gonna come to me with a message from HR to kill you here in this world for the greater good. So you can stay till I get the order or you can run and get pay back or hope that a solution presents itself before the current ones catch up to you." Mr Bill was being as sincere and honest as he could to his old friend and coworker.

"ARE YOU SERIOUS! After all I've lived through and done for our people, it's to be killed. I can never go home or even be attempted to be cured?" Mr Bill turned around to answer Mr Frank. But he had already blinked himself to somewhere else on this earth.

"Dam it, I'm gonna have to hunt him down, Mr Alan, where are you?" Mr Bill continued walking around dropping weapons on the ground in front of the MOP soldiers as he went up and down the side of the bluff supplying the assault. He was brainstorming back up plans on how to kill the witch. This battle was all but one the last of the Army on the beach was being smashed to dust with RPG fire and a never halting onslaught of bullets. The horn of another train further south by the arsenal could be heard preparing to leave. Suddenly Mr Alan appeared in a blink right in front of Mr bill.

"Well Speak of the Devil." said Mr Bill. " Just saw Mr Frank, Good thing you didn't take his mission he has 2 gaping wounds from saser like daggers at the hands of the Witches Imps. To which she filled with some magical acid that is eating through the suit. Aether was leaking out the cracks into this world. That means the acid was going into his suit room, meaning…" They both said "Void Sickness" In unison. "Have you heard from HR? Who other than us three knows?" Mr Bill looked like he was tapping a smoke out of a cigarette pack in his hands, only he didn't have a pack of smokes. Mr Alan had noticed his smoking was increasing the more this little mission went on.

"No one has come to me yet Sir, But a breach like that with an aether leak means he can't blink home, only so far around this planet. Hell he can't even blink around this universe. Least of our worries for the moment now Sir, I'm here cause the Witch sent her Battle Mage and he melted my team and blew the explosives we never got near to getting even in the caves." Mr Bill's red orbs flashed back to life.

"WHAT BATTLE MAGE!?! All her coven is away or dead. Who in the hell are you talking about?" Mr Alan didn't have time to get a response or even act mad before the loud deafening roar came from the river valley below.

"Sallos can you and your legions clear the beach and the train tracks while fighting the MOP on the bluff? I also require you to keep Dom alive and safe at all times?" A plan was forming in Lex's head, a plan that might actually work this time, because he had a gut feeling it wound.

"My dear Summoner, We will protect this Prince of yours to the death. As for the beach, it is as good as ours. I take it you have other things to tend to?" He spoke so easy and smooth it put the men at ease. "But before I make our grand entrance, Sir? May I use all my Legions and powers to ensure taking and holding the entire area for say 2 miles round? The Demon Sallos was proving to be quite the Great Duke his title implied.

"Granted Commander Sallos! Please be sure the next train gets through without being slowed in the slightest. I'll get Orla. You'll know when I do. Everyone ready?"

"YES!" Screamed Sallos and his gator let out a mighty roar as it launched itself from its invisible lurking spot in the waters high up in the air grabbing several harpies within its maw as it clamped down hard with a snap. Its 10 ton body slammed the land and shook the earth all the way to the bluffs top. Men fell over on the ridge. Some to their deaths. Rockets going off in their deaths throws as they fall to their deaths. Whizzing RPGs flow out everywhere in random patterns hitting and exploding everywhere.

It bashed its head back and forth sending the wreckage of the train flying into the river and on the back swing sending another car flying up onto the bluff. Where it rolled over and over crushing line after line of men holding RPG's Mr bill had just supplied them with.

Some of the men managed to squeeze some rockets off only to have them explode there with them as the train crushed them and rolled on over and through leaving a trail of destruction and broken gorey bodies. Fires and random explosions laced the bluff area. Men started getting scared and breaking ranks.

The General watched on in horror at this impossible change of events from some distance behind lines with his makeshift tent and stolen women nearby. Frantically looking around him he took in a new horror. Scores of Demonic looking men were emerging from the water in well formed lines fully armed and marching up the beach to the bluff in droves. He looked at Mr Bill and Mr Alan.

The coward of a man grabbed his chained up maiden and went back to get supplies and valuables as well as an A-M20 Machine gun. Then he slipped away in the darkness back the way they came towards his home state deep in the south. Well away from the Central Band and all this craziness.

"Mr Alan I need you to get in the tunnels and draw that dam Djinn out and make her nuke this entire area. I'm going to take some men and leave here to go kill the witch. The second HR says something about Mr Frank then we will hunt him. Keep me updated. Now go!"

"What about the General prevert running scared there?" Mr Alan pointed back at Henry Daniels chicken ass running while towing his kidnap victim.

"If he makes it past the fairy ring alive then I'll find him and make sure he dies in the mud like I promised." Mr Bill seemed amused.

"You don't want the pleasure, sir" Inquired Mr Alan. knowing how much Mr Bill enjoyed watching humans die, especially at the behest of him.

"Mr Alan, trust me there is nothing I can do that will compare to crossing a Fairy ring with a female slave." Mr Bill was done with the conversation. "Stop making excuses and get in the caves and make Orla go nuclear, I want everything here melted! You don't even need humans to do that, just attack her till she blows!" With that Mr Bill and Mr Alan blinked away from the bluff without so much as anyone noticing.

As Sallos Gator's massive claws dragged its huge mass effortlessly up the beach scores of men emerged in ranks around him from the murky river waters. Without commands they broke into groups marching in unison to various areas of the war zone fanning out. With cover from scores of archers whose volleys blocked the sight of the sky above when they crossed overhead. The arrows rained down on the bluff with insane accuracy decimating the lines of men firing volleys of RPGs down on them.

"Glasya-Labolas, on me!" Came the call from Lex as he jumped from the hind leg of the monstrous gator. "Good luck Duke

Sallos! See you soon." Lex waved him and Dom good bye as in that moment Glasya-Labolas picked him up gently and asked.

"Where can I take you sire?" In his rough hellhound voice. He was a fast and able flier of many centuries of skill. Harpies approached them from all angles of attack but Glasya-Labolas dodged them easily this time. He wasn't carrying an awkward truck while being attacked by dozens of vicious Harpies with no way to defend himself. They also had thousands of hell forged arrows picking harpies out the air around them with inconceivable accuracy. "Was I right about Sallos, Sire? Only demon I know who is still fully an angel." They did a quick dive and spun in the air straight for the rock and moss wall. Lex was screaming.

"Yeeeeesssss! Oh! My! God!" A Harpy dove right in their way of the entrance right at the last moment. Lex yelled out of instinct "Throw me at him!" as he screamed this to Glasya-Labolas he pulled his cold iron rod out of its holster in his coat and held it in a stabbing position like a cruel blunt dagger. Glasya-Labolas released him while in a roll for maxim launch.

Lex went flying in what seemed like slow motion at the Harpy that was blocking his way. Right arm cocked back above his head in a stabbing motion. The Harpy screeched and tried to turn to grab him mid flight but Glasya-Labolas threw him so fast and at such an angle the harpy had already lost. The Doctor hit the beast full force rod going deep in its chest cavity and exploding out its back with a burst of feathers and gore. Lex held on as the two became a ball and rolled through the air and right as he thought he'd hit the moss covered wall.

They went past it into darkness before hitting a rock wall and then the sand covered floor of the limestone cave that was hidden in the wall of the cliff. Just as Dom had said. The two rolled as one till they came to a stop as a ball of feathers, blood and sand. Lex pushed the beast off him and lay there a few seconds.

"Hey um...Duke Sallos? Do you think I could have a bow? I was team captain for the archery squad in college." Dom's voice didn't give away how scared he was, he was. He was frightened stiff. Since Duke Sallos had shown up they were absolutely smacking the MOP down. This was giving Dom the resolve to try and be an assistant instead of a hinance.

"My Lord said nothing other than keep you safe, I mean fighting when stuck in the middle of battle it's a man helping to keep himself safe, no?" Came Duke Sallos' response as he handed Dom a quiver and ornate Hell forged bow. A weapon so well crafted Dom had nothing to compare it to in standard. "My new friend Dom. The quiver will not run out of arrows, So have fun. My only condition is to not leave from the seated position behind me on this gator. Agreed?"

"Yes, Duke Sallos." With that Dom started letting arrows fly at aerial targets that were above and ahead of the great war beast they rode. Sallos noted with amusement how accurate the old human man was. Up rose Deinosuchus with a mighty roar and used its massive feet to clear the train wreckage and debris from the tracks. Some pieces it grasped in its maw and would pull its mighty head back in a swing before launching it up onto the bluff above to cause havoc among the remaining assaulting MOP men.

Lex untangled from the feather and organ filled mess he was glued to. He Stood up holding a fresh gash in his left arm with a hand that still grasped the bloodied rod. He did some quick spellcraft to call witch light around to see the area of the caves. On the wall next to him caved deep in Runic was the word Orla's Run. He looked at the fresh wound and it was bleeding immensely. He placed his hand back over it and started to perform Rieki on himself. The rod is still in that hand. As he chanted the rod started vibrating and humming. Suddenly a bright yellow beam of light shot out the tip of the rod and across the tunnel into the wall to blast into sparks. Lex jumped back.

"What the What?" There was no damage left by the blast, in fact the plant life where the beam met the wall was healthier and grew twice in size. He looked at his wound. No more than a scar now. He held the rod at eye level. "Aren't you full of surprises?" A smile wider than his face formed. He turned inward to the cave and ran full speed Ajax in tow silent as death.

Chapter Eighteen: The Tower

Mr Bill blinked into existence in the shanty little medical tent where Isaac was moaning in pain on a stretcher dying slowly. Mr Bill stood over him and looked up and down at him.

"Tisk Tisk, you didn't do that favor I asked. I'm thinking I might …." Mr Bill started to nudge the man real hard. "Hey you little shit can you hear and understand me? It's the goddamn devil you made a deal with." Mr Bill slammed a fist down on Isaac's rib cage hard. A scream from the guards in the room came at him.

"You stop or I'll shoot!" Said the 1st guard.

"Touch him again and the four of us will be forced to end you sir!" Yelled another. The other two guards backed up and started to duck low and close to the ground. "Hey what are you men doing, stand up and remove this man from the Medical." The officer yelled over to them as they hid closer and closer to the ground almost flat now.

"Try to remove me, you piece of shit." Mr Bill said then punched Issac in the face. Which extracted a loud response of 'Yes I heard you' from him. Followed by crying and moaning. The two standing guards opened fire on Mr Bill; all of their bullets hit Mr. Bill in his upper body. He barely even moved. The bullets looked like they were entering a pool of black water leaving rippling effects across his body as they entered. "Thank you, I've been waiting to get to do this all day." the bullets came out at the trajectory and speed they came in at only in the direction they came from. The two guards dropped without ever knowing how.

"Listen up you two brave living men in the corners get up and get over here." Mr Bill started dumping supplies out his hands in piles on the floor next to Isaac's cots. "Isaac, you want to die here or would like these men to make you into a massive explosive bomb strapped with all kinds of shrapnel and gas canisters I collected from military wars of the many decades? Then I will take you right to Junior and the witch protecting him and everyone else? You can say some badass one liner and rip the cord and take that bastard with you. Or I can kick this cot over and make sure you die of mushroom poisoning in the mud." Mr Bill started his cigarette smoking routine while the bluff shook and the noise of the battle intensified outside. The remaining guards approached silently and started looking through the pile of everything from tape and nails to explosives and saran gas canisters.

"HOO YA! Let's get these bastards for what they did to us." Then Issac passed out again. The guards looked up at Mr Bill.

"You heard the man. Don't worry about weight, just functionality and intensity, ok?" I can carry a bus. So just make sure he can blow a few city blocks away, I'll come back real soon to get him." With that Mr Bill blinked out.

Hundreds of yards below in the cave system Mr Alan was setting the outer wall of the collapsed cave with bundles of explosives to reopen the cave system to the battle on the beach. Behind a light was growing in the tunnels and approaching fast. Mr Alan was reaching to ignite the line of bundles when from behind he heard footsteps. He turned to see Lex holding out his rod with one hand a card in another and witch light of interchanging purple and red lighting the area around him up. His eyes glowed an intense purple.

"How the Hell did you even find me again? If you make one move wizard I'll light these and you will be blamed and that thing behind you will kill you and everyone behind this wall when it's open." Mr Alan said this all very convincingly. Right as the massive chamber was filled with orange light from the entrance of the ball of smokeless fire. Orla had arrived. Neither turned to look for she was already speaking.

"That creature in front of you is pure evil, The Rod you hold can act as a Saser. I felt you heal yourself with its abilities through your Reiki chant, young human, I know that Rod I gave it to Evelyn Knight to hunt these exact monsters many years ago. Sasers are the only weakness these creatures have in this world. Why are you here and why shouldn't I kill you both? Who fights on my beach? Speak or die?" No one moved frozen in place, the power of the voice kept all motionless for moments.

"Lady Rivers sent me to get you back to her safely, These monsters have joined certain men to destroy the world , a comet has cast the world into dark ages again." Lex called for Baal as he watched the room getting brighter feeling that Orla prepared to blast them dead.

"Orla NO! It is The Great King Baal! I have come to get you. I found your family" The demon was materializing as the words were being spoken. His form was that of his three heads on the body of a large spider. He was huge in size, large enough to rival the size of Orla.

"Baal, how are you, my old friend? still a captive to sorcery I see. What is this of my Family? They were bottled up by Silas Mason centuries ago and lost to time with him. I searched for eons. And of this Battle, leave me to rest" Orla changed shape to a red haired woman of no desript features, she had celtic tattoos flowing in spirals all over her skin and wore a long white flowing dress. Baal changed to his Male form and of similar size and they walked towards each other. Mr Alan made a sudden movement and it startled Lex. Lex swug on him with the rod pointed at him chanting one word with power instinctively from his Reiki training.

"RAKU" the chant curled the cavern and shook the cave a jagged bolt attuned to healing shot forth from the rod's hollow point and zig zagged its way to Mr Alan. Nailing him square in the left hip and blowing wide that leg. It flew away and into a billion shattered pieces. A cloud of aether exploded into the area. Mr Alan fell over gripping the huge chunk of missing area his unnatural screams caused Lex's eyes to bleed. Then Mr Alan blinked out the reality.

"What the Hell Doctor? That was downright diabolical. I thought Rieki was for healing." Baal was smiling and clearly knew something about what happened that Lex did not. "Orla may I introduce Dr. Lexington Knight, Evelyn Knight's son. and current Demon Tarot summoner." Baal had a shit eating grin on his face.

"It is a pleasure to meet you, Lex. I loved your mother very much. Don't listen to Baal. Shadow people are evil, Sasers blow their suits apart but due to the negative nature of their beings and the fact they feed off it. Positive emotions and feelings, things that heal. Like Rieki, they have the exact opposite effect on them. What would heal your wound, will make a great wound in them. Do I hear Duke Sallos outside?" Orla seemed eager to leave the cave now. "Ok Baal, I'll join the gang, But I'm going with Dr. Lexington Knight."

Orla shrunk down to a marble size ball of smokeless fire and flew to Lex where she entered the breast pocket of this jacket. Baal and Lex exchanged looks. Baal looked him up and down.

"Where the hell is Rokler?" Baal asked in a disappointed voice. "I gave you a trove of gifts and artifacts, amulets and treasures. I've seen you use a rod and the cards." Baal shook his head and started to fade away.

"What? Who is Rokler?" Baal was already gone.

On the Bluff Above Mr Bill blinked himself in front of the last remaining groups of men. And paced fast in front of the line of men, hands out like leaf blowers just blowing out guns, grenades, knives, rockets and all sorts of weapons from all eras of man.

The men were dropping from arrow fire all around the bluff. Sallos' army started to flank the bluff and ascend the cliffs, while the beach front archers constantly sent volleys of arrows to dot the bluff with death from above.

"Well don't stand there! We have way more guns and way better ones destroy the goddamn beach!" yelled Mr Bill. Mr Alan blinked into a lying position in mud on the ground next to him rolling and wailing his inhuman sounds. Clutching his missing limb.

"What the hell Mr Alan, one had one job?" Mr Bill's red orbs were glowing hot red and floating outside his head. "Blink home man, you're no good to me now." Mr Bill was shaking his head.

"HR wants you now, he screamed. They said 'find and kill Mr Frank then report home.' This mission is a loss." He twisted and wailed. Aether steamed and filled the area.

"Did they now?" Mr Bill leaned down over Mr Alan and reached a hand up and into the hole in the suit where it had been blown wide open at his hip. He shoved harder and harder. Mr Alan wailing and writhing in pain. Till Mr Bill Grabbed hold of something solid.

"AHHHH! Mr Bill what the Hell are you doing to me." Mr Alan tried to grab his arm and remove from inside him to no avail; the pain was too great. Mr Bill was also too strong. He held Mr Alan in place with his other hand simply by placing it firmly on his chest. Slowly Mr Bill pulled a grouping of tentacles all black as the void slimy with aethers dripping off them as they writherd, whipped and grasped at him and the air. As the aethers dissipated and the air was more and more exposed to the growing mass of tentacles being pulled from the suit of Mr Alan they started to change color and shivil up and die away.

Mr Alan's wails got louder and men on the bluff started dropping to their knees or sides doubled over in the pain from the sound of the monster screaming as it was removed from its pocket dimension and threw the aethers and into this world where it can't survive unaided. Before the entire true form of Mr Alan could be pulled out of the suit he went limp from death. A being who had lived since before the bigbang, died in the mud in Iowa.

General Daneils thought he was quite smart and ahead of the game at this point. He had taken off when we knew they were doomed to lose not even those Shadow people could win that. He was resting in the covers of a great mushroom ring. He had his kidnap victim and some treasure with him. As well as food, water and weapons to get back to his village a few weeks walk south. He was pulling her close on her chain while licking his lips.

"Did I ever tell you you remind me of my son's wife? I took advantage of her too, Little shit followed me for years all the way to his death today not knowing I did that." He was laughing and smiling. "I'm a bad guy, I get to do what I want. I'm going to remove pieces of your innocence forever" He was licking her face now trying to lean her to the ground to take advantage of her. A voice came from behind him. It was a soft female voice.

"Can I join in, this looks like fun?" a slider figure walked from behind a tall mushroom. She had long silver hair that faintly shined in the air, Her face was angular and the most beautiful General Henry had ever seen on a woman. "She is very pretty, can I come closer?"

"Who are you?" The General went for this submachine gun but it was a little out of reach. Then he took her beauty in and he was overtaken by her. If he wasn't such a sex addict he may of notice the armor Death Cap was wearing and the poison drips that adorned the spikes fitted around the joints and pads of it. It was dark and her armor was charcoal gray to hide in the dark climate of this new day and age. She approaches him to use her looks and his weakness against him. He noticed nothing but her beauty and his need to have her.

"Come to me my love and we shall take her till she is used up." He reached an arm out for her and made a kissing face. The Mushroom Knight took his hand and with her free one drove her elbow spike and its massive tip of paralyzing poison deep into his crotch. He could barely even make an audible pain sound. She kicked him off the crying woman and with the slash of Fae steel she cut all bonds from the young woman.

"No one will ever harm you again my lady. I am Death Cap of the Mycelium Throne. I wish to take you to the safety of my court and away from this war. Will you come with me?" The woman just shook her head yes please and lay crying. Death Cap made a whistle and two more Fae showed up and lifted her up and off to be escorted to the underground kingdom to live in peace for the rest of her days. Death Cap placed her signature helmet on and turned to face the terrified General.

"I'm a good Fae, I get to do what I want. I'm going to remove all your limbs, I mean ALL" She gestured to his crotch that she had just stabbed. "And your eyes. I'm then going to heal the wounds so you can live the rest of your life out. I will also have my men return you to your home village like this. So all there will know what awaits men like you in the Central Band." Death Cap slowly stalked towards him, the skull painted on her helmet appearing to be smiling. Tears were all Henry Daniels could produce in return to what was going to happen to him.

"So Sallos and his legions have the beach? Do you trust me, son of Evelyn?" There was a devilish tone to Orlas disembodied voice. A blast of intense heat struck the ceiling of the cave and blew a hole straight through to the bluff above. Orla levitated the Doctor before he could say yes through the new entrance and in the middle of the area above. He found himself surrounded by MOP men grasping at weapons of all sorts and frantically moving to and fro as arrows landed all around. Everything froze. A few arrows hit Lex and bounce right off.

"Holy shit the seal of Solomon works. Just not with rock walls" Lex rubbed his arm and looked around at the surprised men and reached into his bag of pouches, he just started grabbing them randomly. Ice Wall. He read the spell craft then threw it behind him without looking. A large wall of 5 foot thick ice formed 12 foot high and 30 feet long effectively covering his entire rear. The MOP's surprise wore off and they started opening fire. Their onslaught of rockets, grenades and bullets had no effect, they exploded and bounced off not even registering with Lex as anything more than a nuance.

"Dr. Lex, I can melt them all in one blast if you like?" Orla's melodic voice said from his pocket. Lex shook his head no. he pulled another pouch out. His eyes burned brighter than ever. Electric Storm. He read the spellcraft and threw the pouch at men to his right. The storm of lighting fried dozens of men to smoking lifeless bodies in an instance. He turned to look at the remaining men. They were running off in all directions.

Mr Bill, having seen Lex's entrance unfold while ripping the entity of Mr Alan from existence, blinked back to the medical tent to get Isaac.

"Is he ready?" Asked the impatient and foul smelling Mr Bill. Something the guards noticed. The Shadow people never had a smell ever. And somehow Mr Bill stunk of some ungodly stench. It was dripping from his arm. Both men nodded yes eagerly. "Ok Issac I can only blink you so far and it's gonna hurt a lot. But when we land we will be close enough for you to pull the switch and blow all your enemies and failures away." Before Isaac could react Mr Bill grabbed him and they blinked away. The two men left hit the ground like sacks of dead weight with relief.

"Well Orla shall we go see Lady Rivers then?" Lex sat down in the mud in a heap of exhaustion watching the few remaining men run away, some of them occasionally being felled by an arrow or two. Sallos' men flank groups were on both sides of the bluff tops now and closing ranks. It was over here. They had won the day. "Let's meet with Sallos, Baal and Glasya-Labolas first, My brother's train must leave straight away." Lex continued sitting there in the mud breathing.

"Of Course Lex, Whenever you are ready." Orla was humming a gaelic tune and Lex found it soothing. A train horn came screaming through the air as a high speed train could be seen and heard below. The young Cameron just jacking down repeatedly on the horn over and over as it sped by at breakneck speeds. Lex looked with tears filling his eyes and running down his face.

"Safe travels Brother." Lex only ever cried like this once, when his mother died.

On the beach below Harpies were dive bombing Sallos and his men. Many of the harpies slammed into the ground or water dead riddled with arrows as the area had near a thousand or two men spread for a distance and then some. Deinosuchus the mighty gator was lunching and clasping down on several harpies at time in mid flight. His two riders Sallos and Dom lashed out at others with spear and bow. Glasya-Labolas came swapping by with his wide wing span and huge back. A smaller yet muscular 90 pound silhouette of a wolf on his back.

Ajax used his jaws to maintain a hold on the wild diving demon as he bobbed and weaved through the aerial battle clawing harpies that came too close. He suddenly roared back and then forward. Ajax released his jaws from the nape of Glasya-Labolas neck and was flung forward into the back of a harpy about the swope on Dom and Sallos from behind. Ajax hit the harpy with maw open and serrated teeth flashing. The force of the blow behind Glasya-Labolas throw was so great Ajax bite the harpies head clean off and surfed its lifeless body towards the river below.

Dom caught sight of the event with amazement at the pure focus of the familiars skill.

His mind started to think how I can help save Ajax from the rush of the river. Before his thought ended and Ajax even came to hit the black water Glasya-Labolas swooped in under him. Ajax leaped from the corpse of his enemy and on the back of his ally Glasya-Labolas where bit down on his neck and they turned hard back around to cover the men on the gator. Dom blushed at his ignorance in thinking he could help either of these magical creatures in any other way then continue to kill as many harpies as he can on his own.

Chapter Nineteen: The World

Lady Rivers sitting crossed legged in the air floating next to the lit fire of the middle cauldon pit. Her grand dagged dress and overcoat hanging low almost to the ground her arms were out and clasping those of her friends on each side. Pairlut and Szuil. Tens of dozens of Imps,spirits, Fae and familiars of a vast variety, all occupants of River Manor gathered around. Many freshly awoken from their rest inside their tailesmens, amulets and special magical homes and hideaways that the Coven of River Manor tend to over the centuries. Many are friends, familiars and family of past, present and future Coven Members. A few are political refugees, asylum seekers and lost souls in need of help. All are mourning the losses and damage to their home and Family. They sat around the fire holding hands and singing. Mr Bill blinked into the sand pit circle adjacent to them with a groaning and equipment strapped Issac.

"Issac you little shit I completely missed the goddamn front yard." Mr Bill tossed Issac to the sand with welp and clank of canisters. Mr Bill started to act like he was packing smokes against his hand. "Greeting Lady Rivers and company, We simply want Junior" He lied, lifting his hands to his featureless face like he was actually lighting and inhaling a long drag off a cigarette. Many of the group looked around confused. While Pairlut and Szuil already had humming daggers in hand and stalked their way in two different directions through the crowd unseen. Someone started clapping. It was Lady Rivers

"Hatman! How have you been, you sadistic bastard?" Lady Rivers was floating towards him a glowing ring of runes in a circle below her. Orion the cosmic snake slipped out her cuff onto the ground and slithered around the middle caulon pit and all its occupants he was growing longer in length as he went. Seemingly unnoticed by all. Krip popped from his hiding spot and had a pouch he was tossing up and down in his hand while smiling like he was a child who wanted to play baseball. A little scoreboard popped up behind him in magic witch light he created. It was home 2, Away 0 written on it. The horns of the old river bandits baseball stadium downtown went off right then like a game had been won. Mr Bill cocked his head at the little Imp.

"Well if he is the most impressive little shit ...if I.." He turned his head to the stadium and back to Lady Rivers and Krip. "You gave void sickness Mr Frank didn't you? I'm not even mad. That shit made my whole day right there. The baseball thing....coolest thing ever." Mr Bill kept smoking his nonexistent smoke. Lady river floated past Mr Bill and to Issac.

"What has this creature done to you child?" Issac started crying. He was bundled up in explosives and canisters of gas and poisons. His face and right hand are the only thing exposed and not bound tightly. His face was half melted away with most of his jaw and its bone showing. His eye lids were as well as a lot of loose skin areas that had been fully cutaway. "Issac, I see the trigger in your hand. Please release it. I will heal you as best I can. When you're healed you can leave River manor and go do what you must then, but don't be this creature's toy any longer." She was holding his face softly with one hand and leaned in to kiss his forehead. "Sleep"

Isaac was out cold instantly. Lady Rivers rose up and turned to face Mr Bill. He was gone. He had blinked out of there the second she took eyes off him. He realized when he had discovered where he blinked into that his plan was doomed. When he saw the cosmic snake orion wrap a circle around all the inhabitants as well as her golden circle of protection and ease of attitude with him there, he knew he lost that attempt.

Lex was walking in the sandy mud with some difficulty talking casually with Orla who floated alongside as a baseball sized orb. The scene they came upon was grisly and at the same time heroic. Sallos was petting the neck of his mighty gater who was shredding a 5 meter cat fish into strips of flesh on a large sheet of metal. Ajax was nearby tearing into a catfish piece with ferocity. Dom was sitting with Ajax petting him and exchanging conversation with Sallos. They seemed to be enjoying themselves. Glasya-Labolas lay near Ajax similarly devouring a large strip of catfish. Sallos' men stood in ranks for as far as they could in all directions. Either eating or waiting to eat. Scanning the field more Lex noticed several more catfish carcaces. Baal Turned to Orla and Lex.

"We won today, but this is far from over. In Salem, The Closing Dawn built Jade Towers and controlled the waters and air. Orla, Silas Mason has built a temple city over Salem to rival the ones of old. He uses Djinn to power the towers, He breaks through to the sky and the sun is there. Orla, Two of the Djinn are your Husband and Son." Orla's howl was the purest fury ever to be heard by any present that day. She had converted to her female form by then. She was trembling uncontrollably.

"Where is Lady Rivers?" Orla looked ready to blow.

"Orla listen, we are all going with you to get them." Came Baal's response. Lex pushed Baal away.

"She is at River Manor awaiting you, please wait for me at the Manor before you leave!" shouted Lex. His eyes teared up. "When will I see my Brother Baal?" Lex turned and walked away towards the group near the water eating catfish.

Further down river a blind choking man tried with no success to pull himself from the river. Suddenly a dark cracked aether leaking arm reached in and pulled him out and on to the bank. The aether streaming from Mr Frank had found junior west of the QCA. Neither was in good shape. Junior was heavy and puking filthy river water over and over. Some of it into Mr Franks seething wound on his forearm. Starting a fresh batch of aether steam. Mr Frank held Junior tightly.

"Got you my dude." he said in a deeply pained voice. "Have you seen yourself you look like shit? What you can't see, here feel around with your hands" Mr Frank grabbed the fleshless hands that were juniors and pushed the bone fingers around his face and started a huge fit of maniacal laughter. Junior began to start what could only be described as what was crying for him now. This sent Mr Fank into a whirlwind of laughter. "Now this isn't too bad a way to die." Mr Bill blinked into the party and the mirth left Mr Franks' voice and he froze there holding the rolling around fitful Junior. "I was just starting to have fun."

"Look Mr Frank, Mr Alan is dead so no HR mess till I go back. If you and the skeletor here take the stuff oozing out of those void wounds and humans drink it, it will change them." Mr Bill leaned in and started poking Junior. "Jesus man have you seen yourself?" he shook his head and looked back at Mr Frank. "So here's the deal, I'll go home, your suit room gets unplugged from the grid, you live here, breed monster shadow people race and then get revenge on the river manor. I'll be coming back with a team but from the East coast since they got Orla. But Mr Frank. Make an Army, HR is going to send a slender." Mr Bill kicked Junior in the balls and blinked off before any questions could be had. Mr Frank Pushed junior off him and suddenly started pushing wave after wave of supplies out his void armor before it was to be unplugged from the grid. Guns, explosives, bandages, drugs and any supply you could think of was piling up all around as Mr Frank let off a fierce howl.

Back at River Manor things were solem. Reconstruction of the Manor was amazingly already underway considering more then 100 Imps were now awake and working at cleaning, rebuilding and setting up temporary tents for staying in along the property. The main fire pit was the sight of chefs and cooks making meals for the mass of workers and familiars all now active. A level of activity that was bound to only increase.

Lady Rivers, Dom, Duke Sallos, Baal and Dr. Lexington Knight all sat in the sand pit in a circle of chairs discussing the future of the Manor, The Coven, and the much needed mission to Salem. But the conversation had changed to Baal asking for another demon to be brought forth and plans to start to build the area up on top of everything else.

"Asmosday should be brought forth and his legions so we can start to build the Pyramid complexes on the river. When we return from Salem with the Magicians power and the Freed Djinn will have all we need to activate them, an usher in the 2nd golden age of mankind." Baal's little speech had such vigor behind it.

"This King of Demon Princes is not lying my Lord. Pyramids are what they seek to build themselves. Silas Mason is starting in Salem simple because he is building his armies which are arriving from overseas to his port, as we speak. Eventually The Closing Dawn will come for this river to complete exactly what Baal is proposing. We should be stopping them and building the future for the people of earth right and make it free, Not let a tyrant like Silas Mason do it." Duke Sallos was dead serious. Lex and Lady River sat next to each other and were sharing grim looks.

"The Closing Dawn and Sila Mason are the magicians who took over the area and built the Jade pillars and new city of Salem somehow over flooded lands? Where do they use strange magic to break the cloud barrier and the sun shines once more?" Lex was just repeating what he had been told this evening to recap for himself, the Demons were nodding at him. "They wish to build a pyramid complex on the river here because it flows east to west, has a strong limestone base, in the middle of the county, it's Basically like he is going to build his version of the Giza plato? here to rebuild mankind? Only instead you want me to do it, well us to build it.. I have to sleep on all this. Thank you everyone. All get rest, we will meet again soon." Lex stretched and looked around his gut feeling screamed louder than ever at him. He knew what to do. It was the right thing to do. It would work out for everyone in the Central Band that needed them. It just wasn't going to work out for Lex. "Baal, who is Rokler?" He yelled to Baal as the Demon King was walking with Sallos towards the hill and the Arsenal where their new duties lay.

"Doctor, I gave you and your Brother many gifts the night we met. The cards being the least of them." Baal turned to Sallos grinning. Sallos nudged the old demon.

"The Knight brothers have your worldly gifts? Like Rokler?" a wide grin on Sallos' face. "If anyone deserves Rokler it's The Knights of Baal." Sallos and Baal Laughed deeply.

End Of Book One

Made in the USA
Middletown, DE
06 June 2022